S0-BYA-931

V

. . . for Victory!

I stole a sidelong glance at Michael and wondered what I had done to deserve this magnificent man as a dinner companion. The rest of the evening was perfect. The handsome detective was by turns funny and shy, and seemed to get better looking as the night wore on (I wasn't drinking, by the way). But the truth is, I'm not ready for a relationship. Seriously. No, really. I'm not. I mean it.

Michael insisted on walking me to my Jeep. I felt the heat radiating off his hands as he slowly drew the belt across my body and clicked the buckle into place. "It's the law, you know," he said, staring at me.

"Thank you, Officer." My lips tingled under his gaze.

He was still staring at my mouth. "Can I call you?"

When I got home I found a new message on my machine. . . .

'Til next time,

V

"You'll absolutely love V—in fact, you'll wish you were her friend. But since that can't be arranged, you'll happily settle for reading her diary and discovering her most private thoughts and all the outrageous things that happen in her life."

—Kate White, editor-in-chief, *Cosmopolitan*

ALSO BY DEBRA KENT

The Diary of V: The Affair
The Diary of V: The Breakup

THE DIARY OF

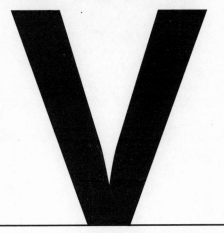

Happily Ever After?

DEBRA KENT

WARNER BOOKS

An AOL Time Warner Company

Copyright © 2001 by Women.com LLC

All rights reserved. No part of this book may be reproduced in any form or by any electronic or mechanical means, including information storage and retrieval systems, without permission in writing from the publisher, except by a reviewer who may quote brief passages in a review.

Cover design by Diane Luger

Book design by Stanley S. Drate / Folio Graphics Co., Inc.

Warner Books, Inc.
1271 Avenue of the Americas
New York, NY 10020

For more information on Time Warner Trade Publishing's online publishing program, visit www.ipublish.com.

 An AOL Time Warner Company

Printed in the United States of America

0-7394-1959-5

For Jeff

Acknowledgments

Chronicling the life of Valerie Ryan was a solitary endeavor, yet the final product wouldn't exist without the help and support of many good people.

Deepest gratitude goes to my agent, Sandy Dijkstra, whose energy never falters even when her cell phone battery does; Amy Applegate, treasured friend and scrupulous counsel; editor Beth de Guzman at Warner, talented and insightful and funny as hell; Jennifer Woodhouse at *Redbook,* who has kept a keen editorial eye on V's life online; Elisabeth James at The Dijkstra Agency, for her tireless work and for standing at the finish line with comfort and encouragement; Kate White, for launching Valerie Ryan and for her faith in this project; Andy Mallor, for his help with the legal details in Val's complicated life; John Applegate, Betsy Birch, Richard Balaban, Julie Bloom, Lisa Kamen, Carolyn Lipson-Walker, Jane Mallor, Lorraine Rapp, Steve Scott, Linda Scott, Alisa Sutor, George Walker, and Donna Wilber for their friendship; Linda Alis, Mara Lea Rosenbarger, Carole Holton, and Thomas Sharp for their insightful guidance; and Diane Weidenbener for putting groove in my life.

I am inspired daily by Jeffrey Isaac, an exceptional

husband, true intellectual, community activist, and faithful president of the Mark Jackson fan club; Adam Kent-Isaac, who is smart and funny and strong enough to open any damn jar in the house; Annelise Ruiz Kent-Isaac, already an intuitive writer and greater singer; Martha Spitzer, for teaching me that a little lipstick is a good thing; Brian Kent, a true Mac'o through and through; Richard Spitzer, a great musician and really cool guy; Terry and Jerry Coleman, who have found their tropical paradise and are generous enough to share it with me; Hy and Sylvia Isaac, the best in-laws in the free world; and Poe, Coltrane, and Joseph P. Kendicott, for their unconditional adoration.

When we last caught up with Valerie Ryan, she had revealed her philandering husband's secret condo hideaway, busted his bogus marriage to a mail-order bride named Mary, and braced herself to fight for his fortune in a groundbreaking divorce settlement, with the help of attorney Omar Sweet and private investigator Libby Taylor. Roger found another new and excruciatingly young girlfriend, Valerie got in touch with her inner Martha, pulled the plug on her affair with Eddie, and became a local hero when a psychic dream led to a missing woman—and a promising first encounter with Detective Michael Avila.

Now, V's adventures continue . . .

May 14

Overheard at supermarket checkout: "So I said to my husband, 'Look, if you're going to cheat on me, you'd better do it now so I can divorce you before I hit forty. I want to leave you while I'm still marketable, and nobody's going to want me once I'm forty.'"

Spring is here. The air is balmy, the trees are flowering, and I feel fat. Comfort dictates what vanity prohibits: sleeveless blouses and shorts. I always get depressed when the weather warms, because I can't fully engage with the season. Of course I could if I wanted to. God knows, lots of women around here wear what they want with no apparent regard for rippling flubber, and I admire them even as I stare in disbelief. But I don't have that kind of nerve. So I suffer silently in long pants and quarter-length sleeves.

I suppose I could get cosmetic surgery, but with my luck, I'll be one of those horror stories you see in *People* magazine. Either I'll wind up with my ass grafted to my face, or I'll never come out of the anesthesia. I'm not sure which is worse.

I'm meeting with Omar and Libby tomorrow.

'Til next time,

V

May 15

Libby has more evidence on Roger. Hunting through his trash can, she discovered deposit slips and statements from offshore banks. "I'm afraid I'd miscalculated your husband's net worth," she told me.

"Ex-husband," I corrected.

"Your ex-husband." She released a small but sincere smile. "Congratulations."

"Thank you. Go on, please." I was sure she'd tell me that he'd squandered all his money in the stock market. I braced myself for the worst.

"Ms. Ryan, your ex-husband is worth considerably more than our original estimate. Unless I've missed something, his holdings are valued at approximately one hundred and three million dollars. Give or take."

I stopped breathing. I looked at Omar, then Libby, then Omar again. "Are you kidding?"

"Ms. Ryan, you're not paying me to kid around." Libby slid a black binder across the table. "Copies of everything. Yours to keep." I distractedly flipped through the pages. My heart was hammering in my ears. One hundred and three million dollars. That tightfisted philandering bastard was the richest man I'd ever met.

Omar slapped his binder. "Ha-hah!" He was beaming. "We're bulletproof, kiddo. We're going to nail Roger Tisdale for every penny."

"With God's help," I added.

"You don't need God's help, kiddo. I'm your lawyer. That's enough."

Libby nodded her head. "He happens to be right." She slid her file folders into a neat black satchel. I noticed then that she was pregnant. I felt a flicker of envy. She was young and pretty and smart, all that promise and happiness, and it all lay ahead.

'Til next time,

CV

May 16

Got the Zoe Hayes reward check. Yippee. Now I can pay my bills. I found an online diet support group. I read a message from a woman who said she's tried everything to lose weight. She put on seventy pounds with each pregnancy. At her heaviest, she weighed one sixty-one at five foot four. She said the only thing that worked for her was something called Butt Buster by LiteZone Herbals. These supplements actually adjusted her metabolism, so she burns fat and calories more efficiently. I e-mailed her right away. I wanted to know what was in the stuff, whether it could kill me. She e-mailed back. "It's all natural. All herbs. It's not cheap, but well worth the money."

Well, pennyroyal is an herb too. That doesn't make it healthy. But I'm intrigued. I think I'm going to try it.

She said I could order through her. Maybe after I pay my bills. I have to see how much money I've got left.

'Til next time,
ꝟ

May 18

Big Head, aka soccer coach Jerry Johansen, took the liberty of registering Pete for soccer, and given my suspicions about him—that he has entirely too much interest in my son and may, in fact, be a latent child molester—this doesn't make me happy.

"You don't think I'm going to coach this team without our best player, now, do you?" he says.

"That was very kind of you, Jerry," I lied.

"Well, I figured you've got your hands full, being a single mom and all. You can drop a check in the mail whenever you have a minute."

I felt oddly comforted. If he were intent on getting his hands on my kid, would he have reminded me to pay him? Wouldn't he have said something like, "Don't worry about the money. It's the least I can do to have Pete on the team"?

'Til next time,
ꝟ

May 19

I paid my bills. I have nothing left over. I guess I won't be getting those miracle fat pills after all.

I hate being broke, especially in this neighborhood. Lynette's been trying to get me to join a women's investment club. "Even if we don't make a lot of money, it's so much fun to sit around with the girls," she told me. "We'd love to have you join us."

"Now's not a good time." But someday, I hope to have enough money to join Lynette's club, maybe even start one of my own. I'll have to add that to my ongoing list of things to do with Roger's money, a docket that now includes:

1. Buy that historic villa in Tuscany, the one advertised in the back of the *New York Times* magazine. Fully restored. Nine bedrooms. Expansive balcony overlooking ocean. Private beach. Golf course (I'll learn to play). Horses and stables (I'll overcome my fear of massive animals). Indoor and outdoor swimming pools (I already know how to swim). Pricetag: $3.4 million (pocket change).

2. Hire a live-in masseuse. Have a massage every morning and another before bed. Since it would be too weird to have someone living in the house, I'd have to build a separate guest house in the back. But because I

don't really have enough room for a guest house, I'll have to buy the Stropp property behind my house. It's worth about $285,000. I'll offer $400,000 so they can't refuse. I'll let the masseuse live there.

3. Since the Stropp house is too big for just one little masseuse, I might as well hire a full-time housecleaner, cook (Bobby Flay would be ideal), and gardener, who will plant and tend to hundreds of gorgeous flowers and blossoming trees, and a little vegetable garden for Pete.

4. Fly in all of Pete's favorite soccer players for a private party: Davor Suker, Dennis Bergkamp, David Beckham, George Best, Edgar Davids. I'll pay them whatever they want, but they'll have to leave their wives and girlfriends at home. I'll let Pete choose one to be his private coach.

5. Spend an afternoon in Nordstrom's shoe department, try on hundreds of cool-looking shoes, and buy them all. Pay to have them shipped to my house. Have my full-time housecleaner put them away.

6. Buy my parents an all-expenses-paid deluxe cruise to the destination of their choice, and pay a private physician to accompany them in case my father needs medical help.

7. Take singing lessons with Whitney Houston.

8. Hire the best Chinese chef in Manhattan and build a restaurant so this town can finally experience a real Chinese restaurant, instead of those fake Chinese buffets designed to cater to gluttonous Midwestern

white people, the kind that offers white bread and fried chicken wings and Oreo cookies.

'Til next time,

CJ

May 20

I guess I won't be winning any popularity contests among the soccer moms after my gaffe this afternoon. I was watching Pete on the field. Actually, I was watching the coach watching Pete, and was aware of a churning queasiness (aka gut feeling, that instinctive visceral reaction everyone says you're supposed to heed). The look in Jerry Johansen's eyes was adoring, but also predatory. Sitting there on the splintery bleacher, I debated pulling Pete out of the league. But Pete would hate me for it. He loves soccer. He loves Jerry. He has refused to try any other sport. I struggled with the possibility that I'd imagined everything, and that maybe Jerry Johansen really was a kind man and dedicated coach who likes my kid because he's a talented soccer player.

At that point, I decided that ruminating alone was futile. I needed more input. I scanned the bleachers and spotted C.J. Patterson, one of the nicer Mushroom Heads. She was sitting on her portable padded bleacher seat with a big red jug on her left, a knitting basket on her right. As usual, C.J. was dressed like a one-woman Fourth of July. She was wearing crisp nautical blue capri pants, a red sleeveless cotton top, white crew socks, blindingly white leather Keds, and a wide-brimmed straw hat. I called out her name, and she smiled benevolently and gestured for me to sit beside her. She moved the knitting basket to her feet. I saw that she was knitting a sweater, an elaborate masterwork in varying shades of indigo chenille.

C.J. Patterson wasn't a beautiful woman, but she had all the beauty money could buy: surgically enhanced breasts, laminated teeth, a resculptured nose, bottle-bronze skin, blue-tinted contacts. Her highlighted blond hair was tucked beneath the hat, which could mean only one thing: She was overdue for a root job.

"Want a cup of Crystal Light?" I watched her pour the pink liquid into a plastic tumbler. "How are you? It's been forever."

"I know," I said, trying to return her enthusiasm. "It's been ages." I didn't want to talk about Roger or the divorce or my psychic encounter, or anything else she had surely heard about me. "Listen, C.J.," I began. "What do you think of Jerry? The coach."

She squinted at me. "What do you mean?" Based on that squint, I was sure she shared my qualms. I was thrilled to have a sympathetic listener. I moved closer and lowered my voice. "I think he has a little too much interest in Pete. I mean, I think he likes him a little too much, if you know what I mean."

"For your information, Jerry Johansen is the pastor of the junior congregation at our church! You couldn't find a more decent man!" She pulled her knitting to her bosom as if to shield herself from my demonic aura. "You see? This is how rumors get started! You start spreading these little innuendoes and you wind up ruining another human being. Is that what you want? To ruin Jerry Johansen?"

By the end of the game, I saw that C.J. had been joined by Eric's mom, another Junior Leaguer. They were huddled close and at one point I thought I heard C.J. say, "Like she should talk."

'Til next time,
V

May 21

I've decided to keep Pete in soccer. He loves the game, and I want him to be happy, especially now. But I am committed to going to every practice, every game, and every team party. No camping trips. No private locker-room pep talks. And if Jerry tries anything with my kid, I will blow his goddamn brains out, I really will.

'Til next time,
V

May 23

I go out to get the mail, and what do I see? Roger, parked across the street with his surfer girlfriend.

They're staring at me, so I stare back. Then all of a sudden, the girl leans over and dips her head down over his lap. It takes me a minute to realize she's blowing him! He's got his hand on the back of her head as she rises and falls. And he's looking straight at me. Smiling. She lifts her head, gives me a drooly-mouth smile, flashes a peace sign, then goes back to work on him. I walked back into the house and called the police. Told them there was a guy exposing himself in his car. But they were gone by the time the cops showed up. Damn.

'Til next time,

V

May 24

I'm in a great mood. Here's why:

1. Omar had all of Roger's accounts frozen. Except for the money from our old checking account, he has access to nothing. Ha!

2. I just received the second installment of the Zoe Hayes reward money. When I saw the first check, I assumed that the money was being distributed among several informants. I had no idea that I'd be receiving the total $100,000. It turns out that there were no other successful leads. I'm entitled to the full amount, but it will be sent in $25K installments, which is fine with me.

3. I bought the herbal diet stuff. Took my first dose

today. Waiting for the miraculous results. So far, I'm
still fat. But hopeful.

4. Made an all-day appointment at the Indulgences
Day Spa. This will include Swedish massage and hot
paraffin packs, full-body exfoliation, deep hair condi-
tioning, broken capillary zapping, a *gentle* facial (no
squeezing or popping, they assured me), aromatherapy,
manicure, foot massage and pedicure, and makeup. I
can't wait!

'Til next time,

ᑴ

May 26

Oh, God. I can't believe this is happening. I just got off
the phone with Roger. Oh, God.

I had been online tonight, trying to access my bank
account. It was 9 P.M. I'd already spent an hour getting
Pete settled for the night. I gave him a bath. I read *Frog
and Toad*. I played three rounds of war. I read *Frog and
Toad* again. I sang "Sweet Baby James." Twice. I brought
him a glass of water. Then another. Then tucked him in.
And tucked him in again. By the time I got to the computer, I was ready to collapse. Then Pete was at my elbow, asking, "What are you doing, Mom?"

"I thought you were going to bed."

"I can't. I'm not tired. Can't I just stay here with
you?"

At this point, I want to scream. But I've got to hold it together. "No, sweetie. You've got soccer in the morning. You have to go back to bed."

"Can't I stay here? I promise I'll be quiet. Please?"

"No, hon, I'm sorry. You have to get back into bed, okay?"

At that point, Pete starts poking at the keyboard. I'm trying to type in my account number, and he's hitting random letters and numbers, and the computer is making this binking sound, and then it crashes. I grabbed Pete by the shoulders and shook him hard, and this growling, guttural voice lurched out of my throat. "*I. Told. You. To. Get. Back. To. Bed. God. Dammit!*" I felt my fingers pinch the flesh of his upper arms and he winced. He pulled away and started screaming.

"*Ow!* You hurt me! *You hurt me!*" The next thing I know he's scrambling upstairs with the cordless phone. "I'm calling Dad! I'm calling Dad!" he shrieked.

I chased him. "You'll do no such thing! Give me that phone!"

He wriggled under the bed. Then he realized that he didn't know Roger's phone number. He was sobbing now. "I wanna live with Dad! You're a horrible mother! I hate you!"

"Well, I hate you too!" I blurted out. "Oh, God, Pete, I didn't mean that. Please forgive me. Sometimes grown-ups say things they don't mean. Just like kids. We get angry and we say things that hurt, but we don't mean them."

He stared at me and sniffled. His eyes were pink and swollen. He pulled his sleeves and stared at the red marks my fingernails had left. Finally, he said, "I want you to leave my room. Just leave me alone."

I didn't realize it at the time, but Pete had kept the cordless phone under the bed, and somehow he figured out how to get his father's number. Roger called me at 11:10.

"What the hell is going on over there?"

"Nothing that concerns you, Roger," I told him. I wanted to sound businesslike, but I was shaking.

"I'm calling Child Protective Services first thing Monday morning. Do you hear me?"

I didn't know what to say. "Fine. You do that. And I'll call every theater critic at every newspaper and magazine in the United States and tell them the whole sordid story about Roger Tisdale, the decrepit has-been playwright who bought himself a mail-order child bride." I slammed down the phone.

Now I've got all weekend to torture myself with the prospect of losing Pete forever.

'Til next time,

V

May 27

I woke up this morning convinced that Roger was bluffing. Even if he did call Child Protective Services, it's un-

likely that they'd take Pete away or even file a com-
plaint. I know the sort of cases CPS handles—I dealt
with them firsthand when I was an intern at the county
mental health clinic. I doubt they'd have much interest
in a loving mother who (uncharacteristically) lost her
temper and grabbed her son a little too hard.

'Til next time,

V

May 28

A good sign: I've invited Dale and his partner for a bar-
becue tomorrow afternoon. I decided that what I really
needed was a new cookbook. While Pete and Hunter
browsed in the children's department, I walked past
the self-help books and tried not to notice how aptly
they described my life. *How to Spot a Jerk. His Cheating
Heart. Dump Your Husband Today. Surviving Divorce. Cel-
ebrating Solitude. Custody at Any Cost.*

As I was drawn into the magnetic field of that last
book, I noticed a guy sprawled on the floor at the end
of the aisle. I glanced at him and he looked up from his
book and smiled at me. His smile was so warm and
inviting that I was sure it was meant for someone else.
I looked away, absently flipped through the custody
book, then stole another glance at him. He had sleepy,
sexy eyes and the sensuous, perfectly shaped lips of an
Italian male model. A ribbed gray tank top clung to his

tan, well-muscled torso. His jeans were slung low on his hips, low enough for me to see an enticing trail of dark hair leading from navel to the nether region below the belt. He must have seen me eyeing him, but instead of straightening up, he leaned farther back, as if to give me a better view of his delicious body. He gave a quick nod. "How ya doin'?"

"Fine, thanks."

"That's not a bad book, but *Custody Without Battles* is better. Helped me a lot." He was still smiling. "Divorce is hell, huh?"

"And sometimes marriage is hell, don't you think?" I returned the smile.

"Absolutely." He chuckled, stood up and extended a hand. "Mark. Mark Henshaw."

"Valerie Ryan. Nice to meet you." I glanced down and saw that he was reading one of those huge medical tomes. At the top of the page: Managing Genital Herpes. On the facing page: Coping with Genital Warts.

Either way, I decided it was time to go. "I think I hear my kid calling me."

"Sure. See you around."

As I wended my way toward the kids' section, I drew up the pros and cons. Pro: hunky, handsome, nice, single, likes kids. Con: probably has a significant sexually transmitted disease. I extrapolated from this that he's probably slept around, or cheated on his wife; the type of man I'm trying assiduously to avoid. Of course it's also possible that he contracted the disease from his slutty wife. Or maybe he's a doctor and he's doing research for a paper he's presenting at an upcoming panel. (Unlikely.)

'Til next time,

V

May 29

I managed to clean the house using the Hefty method (sweeping everything into trash bags and shoving them into the hall closet). It's been so long since I cooked outside that I'd almost forgotten how to use the gas grill. When I lifted the lid, I saw the charred, curled skin of a salmon fillet stuck to the grill. It must have been two years old. I must add a new grill to my ongoing fantasy list.

I will say this much for that jackass Roger: He was a damn good cook. In fact, I remember this particular meal—salmon in tangy sauce with fresh tomato-cilantro salsa, roasted new potatoes with dill, steamed broccoli, and warm, crusty semolina bread.

I remember that Roger urged me to eat the dessert—rich chocolate mousse cake with fresh whipped cream—even though he knew I was trying to lose weight. I remember thinking, as I lifted the first forkful to my lips, that it was okay to eat the cake because Roger made it, Roger wanted me to eat it, Roger loved me exactly the way I was. Now I realize that he was sabotaging my diet. He didn't want me to look too good. He didn't want me to look better than him or good enough to attract other men. He wanted me fat and sloppy so he'd have another reason to screw around. In the meantime, he was lifting weights and running the treadmill and doing his Ab Roller contraption.

'Til next time,

V

May 30

No one from Child Protective Services called. I guess Roger was bluffing. But just to be sure, I called CPS myself. I told the social worker I was calling on behalf of my friend. "There's probably no cause for concern, unless there's a history of abuse," she told me. "It sounds like she lost her temper. Lord knows, I've lost it with my own kids more than once." After a pause she added, "First Presbyterian runs a really great support group for stressed-out parents, by the way. It's open to everybody, and it's free. Maybe you—I mean, your friend—should check it out."

"I'll pass along the information," I said, vainly hoping to preserve the ruse.

'Til next time,

V

May 31

The phone rang as I was getting out of the shower. "Hello, this is Jeanette and I'm with the Psychic Friends Network."

I was poised to activate my anti-phone-solicitor gadget when it occurred to me that this could be a career opportunity. Perhaps they'd read about the Zoe Hayes discovery. "Yes, can I help you?"

"I understand that you have psychic abilities, is this true?"

My gut told me that this call wasn't exactly kosher. "Who did you say you were with?"

I heard suppressed giggles. Then Roger was on the line. "Okay, psycho girl. I mean, psychic girl. Can you predict what I'm going to do to my gorgeous young girlfriend as soon as I get off the phone with you?"

More giggles, then a muffled sound and a playful shriek.

"Grow up, Roger," I told him.

"Oh, I'm growing, believe me. Right before my very eyes."

I could hear his girlfriend laughing hysterically, and then heard her say, "Roger, you are awful!"

"Why are you doing this to me?" I asked him.

"Hey, you're the psychic. You tell me."

I hung up and called the police. I left a message in

the general voice-mail box. I'm still waiting to hear back from them.

'Til next time,

Ϥ

June 1

It looks like Mom is in the matchmaking business. She called to invite me to Bellamy's for dinner on Saturday night. She said she was bringing a friend, a man.

"Oh, this is a first. I can't believe that you're trying to set me up!"

"Don't be silly. Think of it as a little diversion. You need a grown-up night out. Please don't say no. Please?"

"What about Dad?" I asked.

"It's all taken care of. The nice young woman from hospice will cover for me. Sandy, her name is. I need a break too, you know."

I couldn't believe I was having this conversation. "In that case, *you* go out to dinner with this guy, your mystery man, whoever he is."

"Bellamy's at seven. Get a sitter. Wear something pretty." And then she hung up on me.

I am extremely curious about this guy my mother dug up for me. Now, what the hell am I going to wear???

'Til next time,

Ϥ

June 2

I never registered Pete for camp this summer. God help me. Now I get to put my single mother survival skills to the test.

June 3

These days, there is nothing quite as exhausting or demoralizing as getting dressed. I've got plenty of clothes, but nothing fits. So much for those great DKNY pants I bought on sale last year. One glance at the waistband and I knew they would never make it up and over my ass. I finally settled on my old standby: black stretch jeans, white scoop-neck top, and black blazer for MBC (maximum butt coverage). Putting on makeup was another ordeal. I smeared layer upon layer of concealer to cover the dark circles and sun spots and emerging zits, and by the time I was done I looked like a mime. I wiped it all off and settled for a more natural, albeit hideously flawed, look. As for the hair, suffice it to say that I could probably get a job on the Weather Channel. Who needs Doppler radar? I'd just point to my frizz and say, "Eighty-five percent chance of rain." If I couldn't look good, I might as well smell good. I spritzed myself with perfume and inhaled deeply. It's yellow jacket season. It has been weeks since I last wore any fragrance.

When I brought Pete next door, Lynette whistled through her teeth. "Wow, Val, you look gorgeous." Lynette's house looked as if it sprang from the pages of *Country Living* magazine. I could smell something cinnamony and homemade baking in the oven, and I could hear Lynette's husband greet my son heartily as he ran into the family room. I wanted to live in that house. Maybe they could adopt me.

By 7:15 I was pulling up into the Bellamy's lot. I took one last look in the mirror and decided Lynette was right. I looked good. I wended my way through the people waiting to be seated and scanned the restaurant for my mother. She was at a table in the back, waving happily, but the fronds of a showy palm obscured her companion. I said a quick prayer (God, don't let him have genital herpes) and moved toward the table aiming for a sleek stride. I was afraid to look.

"I'd make introductions," my mother said, "but I believe you two already know each other."

The man stood and extended a warm, freckled hand. It was Detective Avila!

I was stunned. "Yes, of course." I reached for his hand and he pulled me in for a completely unexpected hug. He smelled delicious. He was taller and broader than I remembered him.

"How are you, Detective?"

"I'm better now that you're here. And please, it's Michael."

My mother was beaming like a flashlight. It was surreal, sitting there with the two of them. "How do you two know each other?"

"Through hospice," Michael answered, filling my mother's water glass. "My mom has non-Hodgkin's lymphoma. I went to an open house for caregivers. That's where I met your lovely mother. We started talking and discovered we had something in common."

"You mean, hospice?"

"No." His eyes twinkled. "You."

I stole a sidelong glance at Michael and wondered what I had done to deserve this magnificent man as a dinner companion tonight. He was the kind of guy who looked more confined than comfortable in suits; I enjoyed seeing his big arms strain against the sleeves of his blue jacket. He wore a cream-colored shirt and silk maroon tie, and there were a couple of shaving nicks on his Adam's apple. I felt a pang of tenderness imagining him preparing nervously for his big date.

The rest of the evening was, in a word, *perfect*. Michael was by turns funny and shy, and seemed to get better looking as the night wore on (I wasn't drinking, by the way). One problem: The handsome detective has never been married. And while I don't disagree in principle to the idea of bachelorhood, I also can't understand how a man this lovely can make it to his thirty-eighth year without getting hitched at least once. But the truth is, I'm not ready for a relationship. Seriously. No, really. I'm not. I mean it.

Michael insisted on walking me to my Jeep. After I

sat down behind the wheel, he reached in and his hands seemed to move toward my breasts. I stopped breathing. God, what was he doing? Then I realized he was reaching for my seat belt. I felt the heat radiating off his hands as he slowly drew the belt across my body and clicked the buckle into place. "It's the law, you know," he said, staring at me.

"Thank you, Officer." My lips tingled under his gaze.

"So." He was still staring at my mouth. "Any predictions about the future?"

It took me a moment to realize he was referring to my supposed psychic abilities. "Too soon to tell."

He made a little pouty face. "Fair enough. Can I call you?"

When I got home I found a new message on my machine and assumed it was he. I couldn't have been more wrong.

The message was from Lynette. "Don't panic, but you'd better get over here just as soon as you get home."

We'd arranged for Pete to sleep there, so I quickly concluded from her message that he must have been overcome by a bad case of homesickness. I put my hand on the door knocker, a shining brass eagle holding a ring in its impressive beak. I pulled back on the ring and let it snap against the smooth red door. Lynette opened it at once. Her house had the soft, dim, shuttered-up look of a home and family unaccustomed to late-night activity. Most of the lights were off and the only noise was the grinding of the dishwasher. "Lynette, what is it? Is everything okay with Pete?"

There was restrained panic in her face. She seemed to be trying to telegraph some message to me through her bugged-out eyes. "What's going on?" I whispered.

"I'm not sure. I wanted you to hear this for yourself."

I followed her into the living room. Her husband and the boys were sitting on the couch, a constrained floral affair with nary a grape stain or crayon mark to be found. They all looked bleary-eyed. I moved toward Pete and he wrapped his arms around my legs and leaned his head sleepily against my thigh ("Mommy's built-in cushions," he likes to call them.) "I want to sleep at home tonight," he muttered.

"Sure you can," I told him. "But first I want to hear what Lynette has to say."

Lynette kneeled down next to Pete. "Let's talk to your Mom about what you were telling me before, okay? And then you can get home and get snugly in your own bed."

Pete shook his head in reluctant agreement.

"Go on, Lynette," I said. "Let's just cut to the chase, please? You've got me in suspense here."

"Well, we were reading a bedtime story, *Knights of the Kitchen Table*. What a great book!" I could tell that Lynette was trying hard to sound lighthearted, which only intensified my urge to scream.

"Then Pete happened to ask me a question. A very

interesting question." She was cuing him. "Can you tell your mom what you asked me, hon?"

Pete kept his head on my legs and squeezed a little harder. I pried him off and coaxed him back onto the sofa. I held his face in my hands. "What is it, sweetie?"

"I dunno."

"Sure you do. You can tell me."

At this point, Lynette's husband led Hunter away. "Too many distractions for the Petester." He hoisted Hunter onto his shoulders. "Come on, chief. Let's hit the hay."

"Pete," Lynette prodded, "remember what you said? About your name?"

"I wanted to know why you named me the same thing as penis and why you couldn't just give me a regular name like other kids." He blurted it out in one breath, then recoiled and shoved his thumb in his mouth.

At this point I was absolutely hating Roger. I had insisted on a tease-proof name, one that wouldn't easily lend itself to some cruel nickname. But he'd demanded we name our son after his great-great-grandfather, some old codger who did something of historical distinction, I don't remember what. Roger was a genealogy buff, and he loved comparing his blue blood branches to the twigs on my own lowly family tree.

"Oh, honey, did someone in school pick on you because of your name?" I asked, thinking it had to be that brat Gregory Martindale.

Lynette held up a hand and shook her head. "It's not that." She leaned in closer. "Pete, sweetie, can you tell your mom what you told me? About the coach?"

My heart clenched violently. I knew it. Damn it. I knew it!

Pete clamped down on his thumb. I gently pulled it from his mouth. "Talk to me. Please."

What I've managed to piece together is this: Jerry Johansen told Pete that his name was also the name of a "very special" body part. "Some people use the word 'peter' to mean penis. Did you know that?" Pete told him no, he didn't know that. Jerry then asked if he would like to see what a grown-up peter looks like and Pete said, "That's OK. I already saw my dad's." At this point, Jerry backed off and said something like, "It's fun to see how peters are all different. It's actually scientific. But maybe we can do that some other time."

By the time my son was through with his story, I was ready to spit blood. I couldn't understand how Jerry found the time or privacy to talk to him. I'd been to every practice, every game . . . except one. I wanted to cry. I'd missed one practice to meet with Omar.

I lifted Pete into my arms—no easy feat at seventy pounds—and brought him home. It was 10:30 P.M. I called Tucker Daley, the league director, who insisted that Pete must have misunderstood. I hung up and phoned Johansen himself.

"Oh, Lord, what kids will say to get attention," he

said, chuckling. "I thought I'd heard it all. But this beats all." He'd worked himself up to a hissing laugh. "Valerie, I'm going to pretend we never had this conversation. No hard feelings, okay?"

"Excuse me?" I couldn't believe his strategy, that lying big-headed bastard.

"Look. Your kid basically lost his dad. He's living in that house with you and your psychic adventures and God knows what else. So I'm not surprised that Pete would make up stories."

I was choking on my rage now. "Look. I think you've got a problem. And you need help. But whether you get help isn't my business right now, Jerry. Right now all I care about is Pete, and making sure you don't get your hands on him or any other boy on the team. Do you understand me?"

"Settle down, now. You're sounding crazy."

I slammed down the phone. There was one more call I had to make. I still had Michael's home number in my wallet. He answered on the second ring.

"Avila." His voice was low and sandy. I knew I woke him up.

"Oh, God, I'm sorry. You were sleeping."

"Valerie?" I was surprised he knew my voice right off. He coughed and cleared his throat. "Hey. No. I mean, that's all right. Are you okay? Is something wrong?"

I told him about Jerry Johansen, my suspicions, Pete's revelation. He promised me he'd check into Johansen's background tomorrow. "I'll make the early mass at St. Paul's and head over to the precinct. I'll call you if I find out anything." He paused. "Unless you want to come with me."

"To church? Or to the precinct?"

"Either. Both. Whatever."

Oh boy. He liked me. He really liked me. "That's okay. We make chocolate chip pancakes on Sundays. It takes five minutes to eat, two hours to clean up. But they're Pete's favorite."

"Hey. Mine too." It wasn't until after I'd hung up the phone that I realized Michael was fishing for an invitation.

'Til next time,

V

June 4

Michael called at 11. I'd been awake since 5:45. I snapped up the phone at once. I braced myself for stomach-turning details about Jerry Johansen.

"The guy's clean," Michael said. "Not even a parking ticket."

"I could kill that creep with my bare hands!" I heard Michael chuckle softly. "Why are you laughing?"

"Oh, Valerie, Valerie Ryan." His voice was soft and musical. "I'm not laughing at you. Please. Don't misunderstand. I just . . . I'm admiring your fierceness. You're like a mama lion protecting her cub. I like that."

"You do? You mean, you don't think I'm a neurotic, paranoid lunatic?"

"Well, that too." He laughed. "Seriously. I think you're great. Now why don't you have Pete transferred to another team and put this ugly episode behind you?"

Eventually I will. But now I felt it was my obligation to let other parents know what the coach had said to my son. I found the team phone list and started making calls. To my amazement, no one seemed particularly concerned. Tomorrow I'm having Pete transferred to another team. And then I'm going to Indulgences Day Spa, where I plan to forget all about Jerry Johansen.

'Til next time,

ᘐ

June 5

Mission accomplished. Pete is on a new team. And after six hours of pampering at Indulgences, Jerry Johansen is just a little brown stain on the wall-to-wall carpet of life.

I have lived in this suburbia for eight years, and among my major achievements, this one tops the list: I had managed to successfully elude the dreaded Klenkastreicher basket party . . . until last week.

I received the postcard in the mail.

You're invited to a Klenkastreicher party!

And beneath that, in Lynette's graceful script: *Hope you can make it!* Lynette had called later that day to ask if I'd be coming. "You don't have to buy anything. Just have some wine, play a few games. Bring Pete. He can play with Hunter. I've got a sitter."

How could I say no? Lynette, who dutifully watched Pete whenever I asked, who helped me unearth Roger's gold with her trusty fencepost digger, who is always there with sympathetic ear and tray of fresh-baked brownies . . . How could I say no? But what, exactly, did she mean by GAMES???

I showed up tonight in the closest thing I had to suburban chic: a red and white striped Liz Claiborne top, denim skirt straining across my thighs, black platform slingbacks. Lynette's house was impossibly clean; her kitchen floor was cleaner than my kitchen table, and even the windows were sparkling, no small feat given all the rain we've had in the last two days. There were lemon tarts and chocolate biscotti on a red and white checked tablecloth, a pitcher of sangria and another of spiked lemonade and Perrier for the teetotalers.

I was the first to arrive. A wholesome college girl named Jenna met us at the door. She was Lynette's sitter. She was studying to be an elementary school teacher. Lynette had all the luck finding sitters. They never hit on her husband, they never yelled at her kid, they never used the phone or ate all the Milano cookies, and they always came with a backpack full of puzzles and age-appropriate videos and old-fashioned books like *Mike Mulligan's Steam Shovel*. Jenna reached her hand out to Pete and said, "Do you like race cars? We set up the coolest track in Hunter's room." Pete took her hand and smiled. Pig heaven.

I wished I could go up and see the racetrack too. I didn't want to stay downstairs with all the grown-ups and pretend to admire the obscenely expensive Klenkastreicher baskets. I owned enough baskets. I bought them at Target. Six bucks, nine tops. Why on earth would I want to spend $85 on another basket to gather dust on top of my kitchen cabinets?

Poor Lynette. I knew she'd been pressured into this party by Caroline Bacher, who'd been pressured into her first Klenkastreicher party by none other than C.J. Patterson, the Klenkastreicher queen, who, thankfully, was absent at this affair. I helped myself to a glass of sangria and then another. By the time Lynette started the party games, I was relaxed, to say the least.

"Okay, ladies, here we go!" Lynette was holding up a small woven basket, about the size of an ostrich egg. I could see the price tag from where I was sitting. It was $35. "You each have a pencil and notepad. In the next two minutes, I want you to list as many uses for this little beauty as you can dream up. Use your imagination! Don't hold back! Whoever comes up with the most ideas gets a prize!" A low murmur rippled through the group. Lynette reached into a pocket and pulled out a red plastic stopwatch. "Ready, set . . . go!"

I was amazed to see every woman bend her head and begin scribbling seriously, frantically, like high schoolers on the essay portion of their final exams. At first I thought it was funny, but then my competitive spirit kicked in and I, too, was scribbling. "Okay," Lynette said, staring at the stopwatch." Three, two, one, and stop!"

There was a collective sound of pencils grinding to a halt, and a few self-conscious giggles. "Okay. Here's the fun part. Let's go around the circle and see what we've come up with, okay?"

Letha Krause was first to go: "Uh, I've got a bunch here. Tissues, pennies, jellybeans, coins, store receipts, pooper scooper bags"—scattered tittering—"sunglasses, jewelry, dog treats?"

Applause and approving nods all around. "Very good, Letha! Excellent! Valerie?"

By this time I'd shifted to the spiked lemonade. I stood up and smoothed my denim skirt. "Here it goes." I cleared my throat. "Keys, spare change, antidepressants, after dinner mints, keys—wait, I said that already. Did I mention antidepressants? Oh, and tampons and chocolate kisses and batteries and all the little crap that you keep throwing into the junk drawer, and hair doodads and condoms."

Someone made a choking noise and there was the sound of suburban asses shifting uncomfortably in their seats. Lynette looked pained. Then Donna Gold, a willowy redhead I knew from aerobics class, let out an enormous guffaw. "Jesus, that's more like it. Now that's what I call a list! Jesus! Oh, God. How funny!" A few other women giggled politely, but only Donna was truly hysterical, laughing so hard she shook and sizzled like a spaghetti pot boiling over.

After the party (I managed to escape with a baguette basket for "only" $29), Donna stopped me at the door. "Don't you just love these Klenkastreicher parties?" She rolled her eyes. "Sometimes I have to remind myself: Donna, you used to have a job in the real world. You were a productive member of society. There was a time when you actually did something besides toting your children to basketball practice and going to Klenkastre-icher parties."

"And what was that?" I asked her. "I mean, what did you do before you started toting kids to basketball prac-tice and going to Klenkastreicher parties?"

She looked at me. "I forgot."

'Til next time,

V

June 7

"We're on the home stretch, Val. We've got a date."

It was Omar. He'd called to tell me we're going to court Friday morning. I was stunned. It was finally happening.

"So what's it going to be, Val, a Porsche or BMW?"

"Huh?" What the hell was he talking about?

"A Porsche or BMW? Or maybe that's too low-rent for you? Are you thinking Bentley?"

"You've got a great imagination, Omar," I told him.

"Actually, I have a horrible imagination. That's what my kindergarten teacher told my mother. These aren't flights of fancy, Valerie. It's your life. You're going to be a very, very rich woman."

"If you say so, Omar." I hung up the phone and, for a moment, considered his original question. Porsche or BMW? Or Bentley? The prospect made me laugh out loud.

The phone rang as soon as I set it down. "Okay, already. A Porsche. I'll buy myself a Porsche! Are you happy?"

"Delighted," came the smooth, sly response. "As long as you take me for a ride." It wasn't Omar.

It was Diana.

"Diana?"

"That's me." She made a kind of purring sound, a low gurgling in the back of her throat. "So, where shall

we go in your gorgeous new vehicle? Let's see. . . .
Oooh, I know! Vegas! Yes! Let's do Vegas, absolutely.
We'll be those two chicks from the movie. Ethel and
Louise?"

"Thelma."

"Ethel and Thelma?"

"Thelma and Louise."

"Right. And we can wear kerchiefs and sunglasses
and put the top down—you *are* getting a convertible,
aren't you?"

"Yes. No. I mean, I don't know. When the phone
rang, I thought you were—."

"Omar? He's *fabulous,* isn't he? I told you he was the
best, didn't I?"

"Yes, he is; and yes, you did."

"And? Did he get you tons of money? Did he leave
your wretched ex-husband destitute? God, I hope so.
The bastard."

"We go to court on Friday."

"Friday? Fabulous. *Fabulous!* So, what does your crystal ball tell you? Are you going to be outrageously
wealthy? Are we driving to Vegas with the top down?"

"My crystal ball?"

"Crystal ball, Ouija board, tea leaves—whatever.
You're a psychic, darling. I read all about it. You've got
a *gift!*"

"No, I don't have a gift. It was just a strange coincidence."

"I don't believe in coincidences, Valerie. No. Everything happens for a reason, a higher purpose. That's what I believe."

"Okay. Then what's the higher purpose behind this phone call?"

Diana sniffed. "Aw, don't give me the bum's rush, baby. I wanted to see how you're doing. I thought you'd be happy to hear from me. I thought we were *friends!*"

I felt a guilty twinge. Diana was the first person to tell the whole truth about Roger, his affairs, his fortune. But she'd been miserable to me before that, getting in between me and Eddie, insinuating herself into my household as Roger's "research assistant." I never completely understood why her loyalties shifted. This was as good a time as any to find out. "Diana?" I began. "As long as we're on the subject of friendship, could I ask a question?"

"Of course."

"I never understood why you wanted to help me. I thought that you and Roger were such good buddies."

"We were as thick as thieves—when I was drinking. And then I got sober and realized what a dick he is. And what a jewel you are. You are a jewel; you know that, don't you? A gem. A truly beautiful person."

"Did you think you were in love with me?" I had to know.

"I didn't *think* anything. I *knew*. Love, lust, yes. All of it. And I was sober and I saw Roger with a clarity I'd

never known before, and I saw myself—my old self—
with that same clarity and I knew I had to make
amends, and I knew I had to tell you everything. About
Roger. And I wanted to see you happy. Rich and happy
and free."

I took a moment to digest everything. "Well, I am
happy. And, yes, I suppose I'm free. As for rich . . . I
guess you'll have to call me back on Friday."

"May I?"

"What?"

"Call you back. On Friday?"

I took a deep breath. Did I really want to open this
door? Sober or not, Diana still felt like a wolf, teeth
bared, panting at my heels. She was a tight knot of in-
tensity, all nerve endings, as purely sexual as a dildo.
"Sure," I told her. "Call me on Friday."

"Oh, goody! I'll do that. I'll call you!" She sounded
so grateful it made me feel guilty. "Maybe we'll have
something to celebrate. Should I chill something fizzy?"

"I thought you were sober."

"I meant sparkling grape juice, you silly goose."

"Sure, go ahead and chill the juice. You can have a
party."

"Not me. We. I'll bring the bottle."

"Let's not put the cart before the horse," I told her,
knowing how prissy that sounded and wondering why
she brought out the priss in me. "I've got to go."

I found myself thinking of how Diana looked that afternoon at the hotel, lying in wait, so naked, so beautiful and sly.

'Til next time,
V

June 8

I went downtown for lunch, then stopped at the hardware store to buy those stupid globe lightbulbs in Pete's bathroom, cursing the builder for using ten of them in every bathroom. As I approached the Jeep, I could see a parking ticket under my windshield and I was furious. My third ticket this year! I lifted the wiper and pulled the ticket out and stared at the list of violations. Overtime parking. Parking adjacent to a fire hydrant. Parking in a permit-restricted zone. My heart slammed against my chest. What the hell?

Then I saw the note. "Gotcha! Have a sweet day. Michael."

I called him at the precinct from my cell phone. "I'm not laughing," I said, still shaking.

"Oh, Valerie, did I scare you? I'm so sorry. I thought you'd get a kick out of it."

I wanted to stay mad, but his tone, his sincere contrition, worked like a salve on my anger. I softened. "Well, it was kind of cute."

"I can accept cute. I was aiming for charming, though."

"Charming? Charming is putting a flower under the windshield, not a parking ticket with every possible violation checked off."

"Oh, you're right, of course you are. How stupid of me. I can be such a dunce."

I pictured Michael sitting in the corner of a classroom with a big white cone on his head. I saw his broad shoulders and big hands, his freckled neck, the little scar above his lip. "No, no. You're not a dunce." I was filled with a warm, gooey affection for him. I wanted to cradle him, stroke his copper hair and kiss him on the forehead. "What are you doing handing out parking tickets anyway?" I said, changing the subject. "I thought you were a detective."

"When I saw your Jeep outside the hardware store I grabbed one of the PVOs off the street—."

"PVO?"

"Parking Violations Officers. What we used to call meter maids."

"So you grabbed her and probably made her day."

"So I asked the PVO for a blank ticket," he continued, sidestepping my reference to his appeal, "and she gave me one, and, well, hence the note."

"Hence the note," I repeated, marveling at how cute he sounded when he used words like hence.

"Forgive me?"

"Yes, my son, all is forgiven. Say three Hail Marys and call me in the morning."

"You've never been to confession, have you?"

"I'm not Catholic."

"I can handle that," he said.

"Oh, and what does that mean?"

"Oh, nothing. Hey. No more parking tickets. I promise." His voice was breaking up.

"My cell phone's running out of juice," I said.

"Cell phone? Are you in the car?"

"Yup."

"In that case, I'll let you go. I'd rather you drive safe, okay?"

"Yessir!" I said, feeling safe and cared for, something I haven't felt in quite some time.

'Til next time,

V

June 8, later

Went to Lynette's house to pick up Petey and my new baguette basket. She looked as if she'd been crying, then forced herself to perk up. "You didn't have to buy this, you know." She put the basket in a paisley gift bag and tied it with a bright green bow. "I just thought you'd enjoy being out and about."

I noticed a few dirty dishes in the sink, a red flag if there ever was one. "Lynette, is everything okay?"

She smoothed her hair. "Fine, fine, I'm fine." She pulled a crumpled tissue from her sleeve and blew in a quiet, ladylike way. "Allergies. Happens every year." She blew again and stared at me. "I'm fine, really." She gave me a plaintive, please-don't-probe look. I backed off. I took my basket and went home. I called when I got home but no one answered. Went to Josie's for a new pair of shoes. Found a daisy under my window wiper.

'Til next time,

V

June 8, even later

Pete said he hates his new soccer team, and hates me for pulling him out of Jerry's team. He said he would never forgive me.

I started crying, surprising myself and scaring my son. I tried to explain that my crying had nothing to do with him, that I was stressed and tired, that I was nervous about an important appointment.

"What kind of appointment?" he asked, now curious and apparently no longer hating me.

"Just a grown-up kind of appointment, nothing you need to think about."

"With Daddy?"

"Yes, sweetie, your dad will be there."

"Are you going to marry him again?"

"No, sweetheart, Dad and I aren't going to marry each other again. But we'll always love you just as much." Pete frowned.

"Hey." I kneeled down to make eye contact with

him. "You want to talk about this? About me and your dad?"

He shook his head. "Can we have pizza tonight?"

I hugged him and he resisted me, contracting in my embrace. "You know, Pete, you don't have to be afraid to talk about this."

"I'm not Pete. I'm Chad." My son has decided that he has no use for a name that also means penis.

"Okay. Chad. You can talk to me about your feelings. About how sad it is to have your dad go away. About what happened with Jerry. And it's okay to feel mad and sad. All those feelings—any kind of feeling—is really okay. It's really okay."

He twisted away from me. "I don't want to talk about it!"

'Til next time,

V

June 9

This day is finally over and I feel as if every nerve in my body has been peeled away. Skipped breakfast, dropped Pete off with a sitter, and arrived at the courthouse at 9:03 wearing the only thing that didn't make me look elephantine: black rayon top and black blazer, black twill pants with flat front, side zipper (whoever invented pleats should be shot; thank God for side zippers).

"Who died?" Omar looked fresh and clean and smelled like something spicy and cool. His bald head sparkled under the fluorescent lights and he was smiling. I took this as a good sign. "You should be dressed for a party, not a funeral."

"If you say so," I said. (I don't care what Omar thinks, I'd rather look funereal than fat any day.)

"Cheer up, kiddo," he said, hoisting his satchel onto the bench. "This should be short and sweet. By noon you'll be picking out your new BMW."

The room was small and airless, and the wall clock was broken, which I tried not to interpret as a bad omen. Roger strolled in with a lawyer I didn't recognize, and his surfer girl, who had her hand in his back pocket. Roger was wearing jeans, a white shirt, and navy blazer. His girlfriend was dressed in a shimmery pink top, no bra, white leather pants, and black heels. Her hair was pulled back into a French twist and her skin was flawless, luminescent. Her only makeup was a smear of pink on her perfect lips.

Roger didn't look at me. But she did. She flashed the same wicked smile she gave me the day she was fellating Roger out in the new Lexus.

Judge Harry Mendelsohn strode in briskly. He was a wiry, compact man in his fifties, dark hair, small black eyes, grim mouth. "Who's this?" he asked, gesturing toward Surfer Girl.

Roger's lawyer stood. "Mr. Tisdale's girlfriend, Your Honor."

"Get her out of here." The girl looked to Roger, then the lawyer. "Come on. Out. Now." He snapped his fingers impatiently. Surfer Girl slinked away. I was thrilled, but also frightened. Roger turned to blow his girlfriend a kiss.

The judge pushed his glasses up the bridge of his nose and scanned some papers on his table. "I've got a doctor's appointment in an hour and don't plan to miss it. So if you don't mind, let's circumvent the small talk and go directly to the statements. Mr. Sweet?"

Omar stood. "Your Honor, we had a contract with Mr. Tisdale, and we relied on his promise, his promise to fully disclose all of his assets under oath. Mr. Tisdale and Ms. Ryan both agreed to release any and all undisclosed assets. We have learned through extensive diligence and investigation that Mr. Tisdale has sequestered his funds, that in fact he has disclosed only a fraction of his total worth. I believe you have our financial report there."

The judge nodded and gestured for Omar to continue. "As you can see, Your Honor, Mr. Tisdale has been fired by his original attorney. He was fired because he lied, Your Honor; he lied under oath and he lied to his attorney. And now, it is our belief that our only remedy is to enforce our contract. And, in addition, to order Mr. Tisdale to pay all attorney fees and expenses related to the investigation. That is all, Your Honor. Thank you." Omar sat down. He reached beneath the table and squeezed my hand.

The judge's face remained expressionless. He glanced at his watch. He nodded toward Roger's lawyer. "Mr. Sloan?"

"Yes, Your Honor." Roger's lawyer was tall and fit, with gray-streaked blond hair and a strong jaw. I recognized him from a picture at the club; I think he won last year's racquetball tournament. His wife was Jasmine (Jazzy) Sloan, chair of the United Way campaign, patron saint of the local arts council.

"Your Honor, Mr. Tisdale is here today a broken man, a contrite man." The attorney looked at Roger as if he were gazing at a kid in an orphanage. Roger stared straight ahead. "He is a man who has been under enormous stress, a man who has suffered depression, a man who has been on a roller-coaster ride throughout his career, experiencing tremendous success, as well as horrendous failure. Your Honor, Mr. Tisdale recognizes that he made a serious mistake in sequestering his assets, and for this he is deeply sorry.

"But it would be too severe to award the entirety of his holdings to Ms. Ryan. Your Honor, it would leave Mr. Tisdale penniless. Your Honor, it is our preference, of course, that the original contract be rendered null and void. Mr. Ryan signed it under duress, and without full knowledge of its import or consequences.

"If that is not an option, then we believe that the only fair action at this point is to divide Mr. Tisdale's assets. Ms. Ryan would have more than enough money to live in luxury throughout her lifetime. We beg the

court's understanding and consideration. Thank you."
Roger's attorney folded his long body back into the
chair and turned to smile confidently at his client.

The judge checked his watch again. "I have a decision."

The judge took a long, deep breath. He cricked his
head to one side, then the other, like a boxer, and
leaned forward in his seat. "I have presided over this
courtroom for twenty-seven years. And in those twenty-
seven years, I have had seen the most contemptible human behavior, and I have met men and women so
utterly foul and so utterly devoid of conscience that to
call them human would be generous, if not inaccurate.
But today beats all." The judge chuckled, took off his
glasses and swiped his face with a handkerchief.

"Mr. Tisdale. You disclosed your assets and you
swore under oath that this disclosure was true, and you
willingly agreed to relinquish your rights to any sequestered assets. This is your signature on this contract, Mr. Tisdale, is it not?"

Roger nodded. "Yes it is, Your Honor." His voice was
barely audible.

"You are a detestable man, Mr. Tisdale. You deserve
to lose everything."

I held my breath and waited for the "but."

There was none.

"Have your accounts and other assets delivered to Mr.
Sweet in forty-eight hours, and if those accounts are de-

livered in forty-eight hours and ten minutes, I will hold you in contempt, so it would be in your best interest to be punctual. Two days, gentlemen. That is my decision." The judge whacked his gavel and stood to leave.

As Omar turned to hug me, Roger leaped to his feet. "I can't believe you did this to me! You goddamned bitch!" His lawyer tried unsuccessfully to restrain him. Omar stepped in front of me but Roger moved around him, flailing savagely. "You bitch! You rotten bitch!" He sucked in his cheeks and cocked his head back. I watched my ex-husband's saliva hit my sleeve.

"Bailiff!" the judge shouted. "Take Mr. Tisdale into custody at once." A short, burly woman with brassy curls stepped forward, her hand poised over her gun.

"The fact that I'm holding you in contempt does not change a thing," the judge told Roger. "I expect you to make the necessary arrangements with your Mr. Sloan so he can oversee the transfer of your accounts. You've got forty-eight hours." He glanced at his watch. "Make that forty-seven hours and forty-five minutes."

The bailiff reached out to lead Roger by his upper arm, but he twisted away. "Goddamn bitch!" he screamed rabidly, his whole body arcing toward me. The bailiff yanked his arms behind his back and snapped on a pair of gleaming handcuffs. I watched her lead him away as he struggled against the restraints like a wild dog. He threw a malevolent glare at me before the bailiff finally shoved him out the door.

Omar turned to me. I was shaking, but he seemed completely unruffled. "You okay?"

"I'm great," I told him, and it was true. "I'm just fine."

Omar held out his hand. "Congratulations, Ms. Ryan." He beamed at me.

I shook his hand. "Why, thank you, Mr. Sweet."

"Under normal circumstances, I'd insist that you treat me to lunch, but I've got an appointment with a new client in a half hour and I'm afraid I need time to change my clothes."

"What do you mean?" I asked.

He pulled back his jacket to reveal a shirt soaked in sweat. "That's why attorneys wear these things, you know."

"Is that so?" I said, heady, elated. The fact of my new wealth lay just at the edges of consciousness, tucked away for later indulgence, like a slice of chocolate cake in the back of the refrigerator. I wanted to spin around in circles, I wanted to shout to the sky, "I'm rich! I'm rich!" But not here, not now, not in the space where my ex-husband had fouled the air.

Omar and I left the courtroom together, and there was Surfer Girl, sitting on a bench, biting her nails. "Is it over?" she asked hopefully.

"You want to take this, or shall I?" Omar asked. I told him I'd handle it.

I moved closer to the girl, close enough to see that she had a small tattoo above her left breast. It was a heart, and in that heart, a name. Roger. "Yes, it's over. And if I were you, I'd ask Mommy and Daddy to increase my allowance, because your darling boyfriend is broke."

Her eyes grew wide. "What do you mean, broke?"

I felt a rush of the purest joy. "I mean, he'll be lucky if he has enough change for the bus."

I raced outside, hopped in my Jeep, and drove and drove and drove until I found myself by the docks at Lake Merle. There was a ghostly haze over the lake. But for the Canadian geese gathering in the long grass, I was alone. I turned off the engine and gripped the steering wheel and screamed, "OH MY GOD! OH MY GOD! OH MY GOD!"

I let out one long, loud hoot and started up the engine. I thought about all the times Roger had chastised me for spending too much money, for buying that warm winter coat before it went on sale. I thought about the time I bought a hammock for the deck and he returned it to the store without telling me. I remembered how he always bought carnations because they were the cheapest, unless he wanted sex that night, in which case he would spring for tulips or roses. I thought about the time he bought me a gadget for clipping coupons, hoping I'd adopt his mother's thrifty habit. And I thought of all the vacation plans he'd rejected because they cost too much, and anyway, who needs to leave town to go on vacation when there are so many fun things to do right here?

I flipped down the sun visor and stared at myself in the mirror. "Valerie Ryan, you are rich." I started laughing, and then I was crying, and I watched the haze lift from the lake like a shroud and I watched the geese with their lovely long necks and stout bodies, and I felt the warm sunlight on my face and I thought, Yes. Life is good.

I called my mother on my cell phone, and she wanted to know whether I planned to move (no) or remodel (maybe) or take myself on a cruise (absolutely). Beyond that, I had no definite plans. All I knew was, I'd never have to worry about money again. It was an exhilarating and entirely alien feeling. The first thing I'd do, I decided, would be to write a big, fat check to Mary's family in the Philippines. And I'd send a check to the folks who are trying to build a children's museum in town; heck, maybe I'd buy them the whole building. And I'd send another check to the women's shelter, and another to the humane society, and maybe I'll buy myself a new car, and buy a whole new wardrobe and get a tummy tuck, or at least liposuction, or maybe I'll buy a summer house up north and a winter house down south or in the Caribbean, or even in Italy, but I don't speak Italian so maybe that's not such a great idea, but I could hire a tutor or even an interpreter who could translate for me wherever I went, but maybe I'd skip the house in Italy and get something on one of those gorgeous little islands off the coast of Florida.

I could feel my heart racing as I sped home. I'd never

known such a feeling, I swear, and even now as I write this a part of me fears that it is all too good to be true, that I'll wake up and find myself huddled beneath some overpass wearing newspaper shoes and toting all my worldly possessions in a Hefty bag.

'Til next time,

V

June 9, continued

By the time I got home, there was a message waiting from my mother, to congratulate me again, and another from Omar. Then the doorbell rang. I pulled open the door, expecting to see Diana with a bottle of sparkling grape juice in one hand, a pair of goblets in the other. But it was Lynette. Her eyes were swollen, her nose pink and dripping. She asked, "Can I talk to you? Please?"

I led Lynette into the house and closed the door. I gestured toward the living room. "Do you want to sit down?"

Lynette nodded and shuffled in. I noticed that Pete had left his socks on the coffee table. I swiped a dirty sneaker from the sofa as Lynette slowly lowered herself to sit. Unfortunately I didn't notice the garlic press. Lynette pulled it from under her behind, and even in her distress, managed a little smile. "You might need this," she said, handing it to me.

"Probably," I said, then realized with a quiet thrill that I could buy a million garlic presses if I wanted to. Or I could hire a cook. Or I could cater dinner every day for the rest of my life. "Excuse the mess," I said. "This place is a pit."

Lynette waved away my protests with a weary hand. "It's fine." She blew her nose. "Your house is fine. Relax." The high priestess of domestic hygiene had given me absolution. I tried to forget the mess.

"Tell me what's going on. Do you want a cup of tea? A box of Kleenex?"

"Tea would be great. I've brought my own tissues." She pulled a small tissue case from her bag. It was made of calico fabric and trimmed with yellow rickrack.

"You didn't make that, did you?" I asked.

Lynette shrugged sheepishly.

"You're amazing," I told her, and meant it. I've grown to admire Lynette's homemaking skills and realize now that it wasn't hostility that I'd felt, but jealousy born of admiration. She dabbed her eyes and I wondered, What could have transformed this unflaggingly perky woman into a sniveling mess? I would soon find out. I went into the kitchen to boil water, but I could only find a single stale chamomile tea bag. "Lynette, is water okay?"

"Fine. Anything. Nothing. I don't care. I just want to talk."

I returned with a glass of water and sat beside her. "Okay. Tell me. I'm listening." I quickly sent up a small prayer: Please, God, don't let it be that Hunter has some terminal disease. I knew that Lynette could handle anything else, but not that. "Is everyone okay? Is someone sick?"

"No, no, it's not that." She laughed bitterly.

"So what is it?"

"This is very embarrassing." Lynette was staring at my coffee table. I thought she was looking at the dried mustard stain, then realized she probably didn't even see the table. "I don't know where to begin."

"Anywhere." I patted her knee. "Don't be embarrassed. I've heard everything, believe me. I'm your friend."

She blew her nose. "Okay." She took a deep breath. "It's Curtis. He's got this idea in his head."

"What kind of idea?" I asked, figuring midlife crisis. Wants to quit his job. Wants to buy a motorcycle and bike across America.

"Well . . ." Lynette's voice was choked, strained. "He wants to involve someone. You know. In our . . . relationship."

"You mean he wants to see a therapist? That's not so ba—"

Lynette cut me off. "No, no. He wants to, you know." Lynette looked tortured. "You know. It's awful. He wants to, he wants us to . . . swing. You know. Sex. With another . . . Lord help me . . . with another couple."

I wanted to say, That's what you're simpering about?

You want to hear awful? I'll give you awful. How much time have you got? But what I said instead was, "Oh, Lynette. I can see that you're really upset about this. I'm so sorry." She blew her nose hard and started crying again. "But I'm sure you will get through this. Come on. You guys seem so happy together."

Lynette rolled her eyes. "Curtis thinks I'm a loser in bed. Deadwood."

"Did he actually say that?"

"No, but I can tell. He's always turning up with these sex books. Always trying to get me into some weird position. I can't believe I'm telling you this. I feel so humiliated."

I tried to tell Lynette that it's okay to experiment with positions, and lots of people entertain wild fantasies. I suggested that Curtis might drop the swinging idea if she were more open to exploring new techniques in bed.

"Yeah, like the princess and donkey idea? Or the priest and the cheerleader?"

"What?" I asked her.

"Those are just a few of Curtis's sexual fantasies. I could list more, believe me. The aristocrat and the trollop. The cow and the milkmaid. He's got dozens of them."

"Okay. Well, would it kill you to play along?"

"Yes, actually." Lynette looked at me directly. "It would. And it would kill my love for him."

"How serious is he about hooking up with another couple?" I asked.

"Very serious. They're coming tonight. For drinks after dinner. To meet us."

Apparently, Curtis had done his research. He found a couple through the "alternative lifestyle" section in the classified ads. They are nonsmokers, free of sexually transmitted diseases, and relatively new to the swinging lifestyle. They stated in their ad that they wanted to have "safe and gentle fun with a sexually adventurous couple."

"Can you imagine?" She was crying again. "How could he do this to me? I don't understand it. I thought we had a good marriage." She pulled another tissue from the calico case. Her nose was raw.

"Lynette. Just tell him to forget it. Call him at work right now. Tell him to cancel. This is crazy. He's got to have more respect for you than that. You're his wife."

"I can't do that."

"Why not?"

"Because I already agreed to it. Just to shut him up. He's been nagging me to do this for over a year. I figured, he'll meet them and realize what a sick idea this is, and it will be over and we can go back to being normal." She wiped her eyes.

"Valerie, I want you to do me a favor."

"Anything, Lynette."

"I want you to be there. Tonight."

'Til next time,

V

June 9, later

I dug out the old baby monitor and set it up on Pete's nightstand, leaving him with clear instructions to call out immediately if he needed me. I got him settled down for the night and walked over to Lynette's. Even though Lynette's house is just a few feet from mine, it felt odd and disorienting to leave him home alone, but I didn't think I'd be gone more than a half hour or so, and I wasn't.

Lynette's husband looked mortified when he saw me at the door. He obviously wasn't expecting me. He started to say something but Lynette jumped in. "Oh, Valerie, what a surprise. Come on in!"

Curtis glared at his wife. "Honey, our guests will be here any minute."

"I'd like Val to stay," Lynette said, glaring back at him. "Just for a few minutes." Curtis was wearing navy blue Dockers and a forest green cardigan over a creamy yellow tennis shirt. He had arranged his light brown hair to cover his bald spot.

"What's the game plan?" I whispered to Lynette as Curtis prepared a distinctly unappetizing plate of cubed cheese and salami. Clearly Lynette had no hand in the food preparation.

"I just want you to be here with me. They're not going to try any hanky-panky if you're here," Lynette said.

She looked jaundiced and weary. I don't think I'd ever seen her without makeup.

"Where's Hunter?" I asked.

"At my in-laws."

"Does Curtis know that I know?" I asked.

"I told him you knew everything," Lynette said. "He just about shit in his pants. Excuse my French." (I've often wondered how French people feel about this phrase and whether they say excuse my English whenever they swear.)

The doorbell rang and we both jumped. Curtis sprinted to the door. Lynette grabbed my hand and squeezed it hard. I heard a man's boisterous greeting. "Well, howdy!"

"Howdy yourself," Curtis answered congenially. "Welcome to our humble abode. *Mi casa es su casa.*"

"And I'll take the taco supremo with extra hot sauce!" came the rowdy response, followed by a woman's giggling. Lynette stared miserably at me as Curtis led the couple toward the living room. I held the baby monitor to my ear and heard Pete snoring lightly. I couldn't bring myself to turn around. I desperately wanted to escape. "This is my wife, Lynette," I heard Curtis say. "And our neighbor, who was just about to leave."

"Hey, no hurry. The more the merrier!" His was a big, friendly, burly voice, hers was high and mild and tittering. My chest clenched as I realized that the voices were familiar to me. I forced myself to face them. Jesus. It was Melanie and Wade Rosen. I hadn't seen them since Roger and I met them for coffee at Starbucks in February.

"Well I'll be gosh darned! Valerie! Lookee here, Mel. It's Valerie!" Wade was wearing a black cowboy hat, snakeskin boots, and a Cubs sweatshirt pulled tight over his formidable gut. Melanie wore a bright red dress and black suede boots.

I was obviously more embarrassed than either of these two. "Wade. Melanie. I don't know what to say!"

"Don't say anything, sweetheart, just take off your clothes," said Wade. "Heck, when Mel and I started talking about this swinging stuff, you and Roger were on our short list, you know."

Melanie elbowed her husband. "Ho-ney, cut it out. I think you're embarrassing Valerie. You've got to forgive him, Val. He had half a beer before we left the house and it went straight to his head."

I saw the tormented expression on Lynette's face and knew I couldn't leave without accomplishing something. "Hey, Mel, I don't believe you've ever seen my house, have you?"

Melanie looked confused but wanted to be obliging. "No, I haven't. Not since you guys moved out to sub-urbia."

"Oh, why don't you walk me over. I'm just next door. I'd love to get your opinion on window treatments."

"Right now?" Melanie asked.

"Please." I reached out and grabbed her hand. "It'll only take a minute."

As soon as I got her out of the house, I quickly explained that Lynette was violently opposed to swinging. "She did look a little terrified," Melanie admitted. "To be perfectly honest, I got bad vibes as soon as we walked in."

"Look," I told her. "I know you guys are sexual adventurers, and it's none of my business. But wouldn't it be more fun if all parties involved were, you know, into it? I can't imagine that you'd have a good time if you knew Lynette was doing it because her husband coerced her."

"You're absolutely right," Melanie said. "It would be awful. I'd never be able to relax." She leaned toward me. "This was all Wade's idea, you know. He took the classified ad out as a joke. I never thought we'd get this far. We got seventeen responses. And the more we talked to other couples, the more we wanted to give it a try. It's all in good fun, you know. Consenting adults and all that." We were standing outside my door. "Now how about those window treatments?"

"Huh?" I asked.

"What are you thinking. Drapes? Café curtains? Roman shades?"

"I don't need window treatments, Mel."

She stared at me, then knocked her fist against her

head. "Duh. Now I get it." She smiled. "Don't you worry about your friend, Valerie. We won't do anything unless she's one hundred percent comfortable. Okay?"

"Okay. Thanks."

I watched Melanie's plump posterior as she waddled back to Lynette's house.

When I got back to my house I checked on Pete. He had gone to sleep with the lights on and his *Frog and Toad* tape still going in the boom box. I drew the covers up to his chin and kissed him on his damp forehead. He stirred and stared at me with a glossy, absent look. He smiled, murmured something incomprehensible, and closed his eyes. He looked so soft and sweet, and I was so exhausted, I climbed into bed beside him, wrapped an arm around him, and listened to his soft snoring. Just as I was drifting off to sleep, I heard the phone ring. I dragged myself out of Pete's warm bed and ran into Roger's ex-study.

"Hello?"

"I hear congratulations are in order," came the husky response.

"I suppose they are, Diana."

"If it's not too late, I'd love to stop by to congratulate you in person."

"Actually, I was just going to bed."

"Perfect!" she said.

"What?"

"It was a joke, Valerie Ryan. A joke."

I told Diana she could stop by later in the week. And then I lay in bed for a long time before finally falling asleep. The phone rang again. It was 11:45.

"I'm sorry to call so late. Did I wake you?" It was Omar.

"Yeah. Sort of. It's okay. What's up?"

"I've been trying to reach you all day. I've got good news and I've got bad news. Which do you want first?"

"The bad news." I sat up on my elbows and waited and listened to Omar taking a deep breath.

"Your ex-husband lost plenty of money on his tech stocks. And his art investments haven't been so hot either."

"Meaning . . . ?"

"Meaning, you're not getting quite as much as we'd originally calculated."

"Meaning . . . ?" I held my breath.

"Meaning you're worth sixty-three million, one hundred seventy nine thousand, five hundred sixteen dollars. And twenty-four cents."

I started to laugh, and then I was crying.

"Val, are you okay?"

"Am I okay? Are you kidding? Six months ago I **was** reading books like *The Frugal Fanatic* for tips on recycling old bra straps and today I'm worth sixty-three million dollars. I'm more than okay, Omar. I'm rich." I wiped my eyes. "Hey, if that's the bad news, what's the good news?"

"Have you checked your bank account lately?"

"No, not lately," I answered.

"Your money is in. Ahead of schedule. I guess Mr. Sloan wasn't taking any chances."

My head was tingling. Did it really matter whether I received a hundred million or sixty million? Either way, I wouldn't have been turning my old bra straps into luggage bungee cords. I was rich.

'Til next time,

V

June 10

At 7:30 this morning, Wade and Melanie Rosen's car was still in Lynette's driveway.

June 11

I saw Lynette at the curb this morning, retrieving the newspaper. I called out to her but apparently she didn't hear me. I started walking toward her but she scurried into the house. I phoned her, but got the answering machine.

Today I saw a bumper sticker that read, "I'm not getting older, I'm getting blonder." Suddenly, I wanted to be blond. I had to be blond. I will be blond. And not just any shade of blond, but platinum. I called Lauren at Boku. I was in luck. She'd just had a cancellation. She could take me on Monday at 9:15. Yes! I can't wait!

'Til next time,

V

June 12

I dropped Pete off at a sitter and raced to Boku. "You sure you want to do this?" Lauren asked, running her fingers through my hair. "You really want to get rid of this gorgeous red?" Lauren—whose last name I don't know despite the fact that she's been my stylist for three years—raked her fingers through my hair and looked doubtfully at my reflection.

"I'm positive," I assured her. I told her that I was ready for a big change. Coloring my hair would be safer and easier to reverse than cosmetic surgery. My hair was now nearly to my waist. I'd have long, sexy blond hair. I was absolutely ready for this.

"Okay, then," she said, apparently convinced. "Let's get started." She draped a silver vinyl cape around me. "You'll make a pretty blond, Valerie. And I can tell you from personal experience, blonds really do have more fun." Lauren's own platinum was pulled back into a loose chignon. Another blond stylist chimed in: "You'll never have to open another door for yourself."

Then another piped up, "And you'll never spend another Saturday night waiting by the phone."

I stared at myself in the mirror. Oh, I was so ready for this. But three hours later, as Lauren blow-dried my newly blond hair, I knew that something had gone horribly wrong. I glimpsed in the mirror for the first time (I had refused to look until she was entirely done) and saw myself—at age ninety. The hair wasn't platinum, it wasn't blond. It was white. I looked like a cross between Barbara Bush and Albert Einstein. My hair had somehow quadrupled in volume. Terrified, I reached up to touch it. It wasn't hair. It was hay. I wanted to vomit.

"What the hell happened?" I whispered, commanding myself not to cry.

"I don't know," Lauren said, staring at my head. "I don't know." She attempted to pull a comb through the hair and I heard it crackle like twigs on a bonfire.

I told her to change it back. Immediately. "I am not leaving this place until my hair is red and normal again. Do you understand?"

"Okay. Okay." Everyone was staring now, all the other stylists, all the women in all the chairs, the receptionists, the boyfriends, the UPS guy, the manicurist, the massage therapist. The woman in the chair next to me whispered, "It'll be okay. She'll fix it. Don't worry."

An hour later, as Lauren rinsed the dye from my hair, I asked her, "How does it look?" I was afraid to look in the mirror.

"Well . . . it *is* darker."

I sat up and stared into the mirror. My hair was now the color of the bridesmaid dress I wore to my sister Teresa's wedding.

Mauve.

I felt my stomach lurch. It was almost 3 P.M. I called Pete's sitter and asked her to keep him until I got there. Lauren glopped on some more dye and stuck me under the dryer. An hour later, my hair was the color of a dirty penny. I ran my fingers through it. My hair came out in wads. Wads and wads and wads of dirty-penny-colored hair, as resilient as cotton candy. I started to cry.

"I don't know what to say," Lauren whispered, shaking her head. "I am so sorry, Val."

I was sobbing now and I didn't care who was watching. "I've got to get out of here. Now."

Lauren gave me some kind of industrial strength conditioner and a plastic cap. She instructed me to put the conditioner on my hair for an hour a day. "Your hair should be back to normal by Wednesday," she told me.

I knew it was bullshit but I took the conditioner and the cap anyway.

It is now 11:17 P.M. and I've had the conditioner on my head for six hours. I'm praying that tomorrow my hair will be stronger. I don't even care what color it is. I just don't want to lose my hair.

'Til next time,

V

June 13

When I woke up this morning, the plastic cap was filled with hair. The conditioner hadn't helped. I touched my head tentatively. My hair felt like wet wool but was still as weak as cotton candy. I had flashbacks of the hours I spent in Lauren's chair, the way I looked when I caught the first glimpse of myself in the mirror, the way my hair felt when I reached up to touch it. I started to cry again. I couldn't let Pete see me this way. I put on a baseball cap and pulled out the phone book. I found Jan Wilson's number. Jan had a salon in her basement. She was famous for resurrecting ruined hair. I heard about her through one of the Mushroomheads.

It was 7:15 A.M. I was crying when she answered the phone. I apologized for calling so early and, in between sobs, spilled out my sorry story. She took pity on me and agreed to see me at 8:15. I roused Pete, took him to Lynette's, and sped over to Jan's house.

She walked around me, examining my hair. She tugged at it and it came off in her fingers. She examined it some more. "Honey, your hair is dead," Jan finally pronounced. "There's nothing we can do now but cut it off." She tugged at it again. "I think we can save about a half inch off the scalp. It's going to be short." I started sobbing again and Jan kneaded my shoulders. "I know. I know," she murmured.

"Just do it," I told her. "Just cut it off."

Twenty minutes later, I looked like a chemo patient. All the money in the world couldn't get my hair back.

I staggered out of Jan's salon and drove to the bagel shop for a cup of coffee. I was dumping sugar into my cup when someone came up behind me.

"Could it really be? Valerie Ryan?"

It was Michael Avila. Just my luck. "Yup," I said, turning slowly to face him. "It's really me. The hairless wonder."

He stared at my head. "I love it." He seemed sincere. "I think you look beautiful."

"You do?"

He was still staring, now at my mouth. "Uh-huh."

"Really?"

"I don't lie." He was looking into my eyes now. "Where have you been?"

"In court." I told him that I'd finalized the divorce settlement.

"Actually, I've heard. Congratulations."

"Thanks. How did you know?"

"It's a small town. News travels fast."

Michael's pager trilled. He checked the screen. "Crap. I've got to run." He looked sad. "Any chance I can take you out this weekend? To celebrate?"

"Sure," I told him. "Call me."

"You got it." And with that, the handsome detective was gone. Maybe my hair wasn't so bad after all. I didn't feel bald anymore, I felt sassy and edgy and chic.

But Michael never called me. I'm trying not to think about it.

'Til next time,
V

June 14

I called Lynette today. I had to know what the Rosens' car was doing in front of her house on Saturday morning. She finally admitted that Wade and Melanie had spent the night. "You've got to be kidding," I said. "Lynette, what happened?"

There was a long pause. "Sex happened," she said, then giggled.

"Excuse me?" I was sure I'd heard wrong.

"Sex happened," she repeated. "And it was incredible."

"You're kidding, right?"

"No, I'm not kidding. Melanie and Wade were incredible. Funny, happy, sweet. We had a little wine, then a little more, then Wade offered to give me a back rub and Melanie started kissing me and Curt was kissing me and the next thing I knew, we were all in the guest room. In the bed. Naked."

I didn't know what to say. "Is this something you plan to do on a regular basis?" I knew I sounded judgmental.

"I'm not sure," she said. "Maybe."

Michael Avila still hasn't called.

'Til next time,

cv

June 15

He didn't call me today, either. I knew he was lying about liking my hair.

June 16

I feel vindicated!

I just heard through my new friend Donna Gold who heard from one of the Mushroomheads that C.J. Patterson pulled her kid off Jerry Johansen's team. No details, but it had something to do with "inappropriate behavior." On the assumption that C.J. doesn't despise me anymore, I called and left a message on her machine.

"Call me if you want to talk about any of this business with Coach Johansen."

She hasn't called yet.

Neither has Michael Avila.

'Til next time,

cv

June 16, later

I found a message on my machine today. Three words. "You're a bitch." A woman's voice. I didn't recognize it. I replayed the message again. I held my ear against the answering machine. I checked Caller I.D. The call that came in at 9:20 was marked "blocked."

The phone rang and I snatched it up at once. "What do you want?" I snapped.

"Hey, baby. Calm down. It's just me." It was Diana.

"Oh. Diana." I let out a long breath.

"I'm coming over," she said. "I'm stopping at Provence for takeout. How does mushroom pâté sound to you?"

"I'm afraid I don't have much of an appetite, Diana. Can I get a rain check on this?"

"Absolutely not. I'll be there in twenty-five minutes. We're going to celebrate."

Diana arrived with a bottle of sparkling cider and a brown shopping bag from Provence, a tiny take-out place on Union where the counter help is haughty and a loaf of bread costs six dollars. Her mouth dropped open as she noticed my hacked-away hair. "Does this mean what I think it means?"

"No, I'm not dressing up as Peter Pan for Halloween," I answered. "And I'm too fat to be a Holocaust victim."

"You silly goose." Diana reached out to run her palm

over my crew cut. "I mean, does this new hair signal a shift in, shall we say, your romantic inclinations?"

"Am I suddenly a lesbian? No."

"Pity." Diana shucked off her shoes and padded ahead to the dining room in perfectly pedicured feet. She unpacked a crusty baguette, mushroom pâté, tortellini, and two dense slices of chocolate torte. "Incidentally, Valerie, you're not fat. You're delicious." She pinched my ass. I swatted her hand away. I still don't understand why Diana plays with me this way; surely there are enough gay women in this town to keep her busy.

Diana moved through my kitchen quickly, pulling out plates and wineglasses, silverware and napkins. She knew exactly where to find everything and I remembered with a shudder how she had insinuated herself into our family as Roger's "research assistant." "Tell me the truth, Diana," I started.

"Of course, darling," she said, batting her eyelashes at me. "What is it?"

"When you were working with Roger, were you actually working?"

"Umm . . ." She slid the pâté onto a plate and licked her finger. "Yes. Sort of." She looked at me. "Roger didn't have a lot of work for me. But he knew I needed a job. Mostly we just talked. The more he talked, the less I liked him. He bitched about you. Bragged about his latest conquests. Talked stocks." She plopped the tortellini into a bowl. "That's how I knew about the gold. Roger loved talking about money. And he loved spending it on everyone but you."

I was surprised to feel my eyes sting with tears. Diana looked at my face. "Oh, honey. I'm sorry. You're still tenderhearted." She brightened. "Hey. Look who's crying now. Your ex is still in the slammer and he doesn't have a pot to piss in."

"How do you know he's still in jail?"

"He called me, the jerk. He asked me to bail him out. I told him forget it. I told him that he should sit there and think about the mistakes he'd made and get right with his Higher Power." Diana grinned at me and poked me with her toe.

She told me that Roger couldn't pull his bail money together. His father wouldn't bail him out. None of his siblings would help either. And once he gets out in a week or two, he'll be homeless and without a job. He's not trained to do anything except sponge off his parents, and it's unlikely he'll score big with another play. He can't even get himself hired to teach because of Alyssa's sexual harassment charges. Diana thinks he'll probably move back in with his parents. "What a loser," she said, spearing a tortellini with her fork and popping it into her mouth. "Wait! I almost forgot."

She topped off my glass and then her own, then raised it toward me. "A toast to Valerie Ryan. The sweetest, sexiest, and *wealthiest* woman I know. You deserve everything you want and more, baby. Here's to you." She clinked her glass against mine and took a sip.

I gulped down my cider, wishing it was wine. "So tell me," she asked, "what are you worth these days?"

I took another sip, stalling. "Oh, a few million bucks, I guess."

"How many is a few, pray tell?"

"Sixty-three million dollars. Give or take."

"Wooo-eeee!" Diana slapped the table. "So what are you going to do with all that money?" Diana asked. I told her I had no definite plans, but would probably buy a winter house somewhere warm and quiet. She offered to serve as a financial consultant. I told her I'd pass.

"I understand completely," she said, wiping her mouth. "It's not like I've got a sterling reputation. If you need help, the offer stands. And when you buy that house, promise you'll invite me."

I looked at Diana. Her dark hair framed a heart-shaped face and tumbled down around her shoulders. She wore stretch khaki pants that accentuated her flat belly and long, lithe thighs. Her black ribbed turtleneck clung to her slim arms and jutting breasts. She was pushing forty but had the wild beauty of a teenage boy. I fleetingly imagined what it might be like, being with her. I thought of Lynette and the Rosens. I squeezed my eyes shut and willed the images away.

"You know," she began, and I had the eerie feeling that she was reading my mind. "It's not so bad on the other side. You ought to try it."

"Huh?"

"Haven't you had enough of men by now?"

I tried to explain to Diana that I didn't think sexual orientation was a choice, that I have always been interested in men, that even after Roger I am willing to try my luck with men again. "In fact, there's someone I've got my eye on right now," I said. "He's tall and strong and nice and cute—and single." Thinking of Michael made me feel happy and giddy. I wanted to talk about him.

"Is that right?" Diana asked, restraining a frown. "And who is this Prince Charming that has you so captivated?"

"His name is Michael and he's a cop."

"Michael Avila?" Diana asked, her eyes popping wide.

"You know him?"

"Not exactly. But I know *of* him." She looked away. "Ready for dessert?" She stood up and started clearing the plates.

I grabbed her by the elbow. "Get back here," I demanded. "What do you know about Michael Avila?"

Diana threw up her hands. "Nothing. Nothing. I mean, I know he's a bachelor. I know he's a detective. I've seen him around and I know he's mighty handsome."

"You know a lot. What else do you know?"

"That's all."

"Come on, Diana. Don't bullshit me. Is he a psycho?"

"No."

"Is he a philanderer?"

"No."

"Is he a liar? A serial killer? A rapist?"

"No, no, no!" Diana spun around. "Look. I really don't know him. I'm sure he's a great guy." She grabbed her glass and tilted it toward me. "I'm sure you'll make a lovely couple. But I'm still hoping you'll change your mind about men. I would never hurt you, Valerie. And I give the best back rubs."

"You don't give up, do you?"

"Never say die." She grinned. "That's my motto."

After Diana left, I realized she'd succeeded in distracting me from our conversation about Michael Avila. I wondered what she knew about him. It makes me sick to think it might be something bad. In the meantime, I await his call.

'Til next time,

V

June 18

Will wonders never cease? C.J. Patterson called me to apologize. She admitted that I was right about Big Head Johansen and begged my forgiveness. She told me that the coach had quit the team, quit his job, and moved with his family to Wyoming. Then she invited me to her house for tea Wednesday afternoon. I accepted the invitation, then wondered what the hell I could possibly talk to C.J. Patterson about for two hours.

'Til next time,
𝒱

June 19

I met with Nancy Cooperman, a financial advisor with Barlowe Associates. Omar had recommended her, said that her clients include Bruce and Babs Alexander (they own half the county), Elgin Wiley (he owns the other half), and Marcus Osten (owns most of the McDonald's franchises in this part of the country). I still can't believe that I'm now part of this elite club. Nancy sketched out an elaborate but sensible plan, and all but guaranteed that she would double my money in eight to ten years.

I told her I wanted to buy a summer house and she suggested Figure Eight Island on Cape Fear in Wilmington, North Carolina. I never heard of it. Nancy said she'd have a realty directory sent to me at once. What service!

Saw Michael Avila at the bagel place. He was leaving as I walked in. He awkwardly apologized for not calling, said he's been swamped with work. He told me again how much he loved my short hair. I did not believe him this time.

'Til next time,
𝒱

June 20

C.J. Patterson doesn't really want to be my friend.

I figured this out after I had started on my second chocolate chip scone. She asked if I'd consider making a twenty-five-thousand-dollar donation to the hospital foundation. She said that my name would appear on a brass plaque by the reception area. "It's an investment in our community," C.J. intoned, "an expression of your commitment to the health and well-being of our precious community. It's a legacy that will live on forever, a legacy for your children, and your children's children."

I'd done enough fund-raising for the Center to know that you don't just flat-out ask someone to donate $25,000. You cultivate them. You shmooze them. You ask them to join the board, or a committee. This kind of cultivation can take months, even years. And when the moment is right, you absolutely do not send someone like C.J. Patterson to "make the ask." It's an art, a science, as profound as a marriage proposal, as delicate as a butterfly wing. Two weeks ago, C.J. Patterson was calling me names. She wasn't a friend. She wasn't even someone I respected. And once I realized that it wasn't my company she wanted but my money, I knew I had to leave. I stuffed the rest of the scone into my mouth and washed it down with lukewarm strawberry tea.

"Thanks for having me, C.J.," I told her as I gathered

my jacket and bag. "Delicious scones. You'll have to give me the recipe." I didn't say anything about a donation. I left the hospital brochure on her coffee table. When I told my mother what had happened, she said I'd better get used to it.

Michael left a message on my machine. He has two tickets for the ballet this Saturday and wondered whether I'd like to join him. I called back and left a message on his machine. "Absolutely!" I said, a little too enthusiastically, I fear.

'Til next time,

V

June 21

I was just getting into the shower when the phone rang. "Don't hang up." The voice was small, thin, male.

"Who is this?"

"You've forgotten me already, have you?"

It was Roger. His voice was so choked and shrunken I would have never guessed it belonged to my arrogant ex-husband.

"What do you want?"

"I wouldn't be asking you this if I weren't desperate," he began, and I knew the rest.

"No, Roger," I interrupted. "I won't bail you out."

"Wait! Hear me out. Please. I beg you."

Anger rose like bile in the back of my throat. There

was so much I wanted to say. Instead, I hung up the phone and disconnected the wire from the wall.

'Til next time,

$\mathcal{V}$

June 22

I started the day at the mall, and ended with a Jeep full of shopping bags. I don't care if my body is less than perfect. It still deserves to be adorned.

It's been so long since I've dated that I decided I needed a refresher course. I went to the library in search of helpful hints for newly single women and found *The Ten Commandments of Dating.* I vaguely remembered that this book was met with considerable criticism when it first appeared, and as I flipped through its pages, I understood why.

Commandment Three: When he finally calls, tell him you're unavailable.

Commandment Seven: If he leaves a message on your machine, don't return his call for forty-eight hours.

Commandment Nine: Don't even consider having sex until you've dated at least a year.

Is this author deranged? Does anyone actually follow these commandments? What's the point of waiting a year to have sex? Why would anyone cancel a date with someone they actually like? I was mystified. Yet oddly intrigued. I took the book home and plan to read it tonight.

'Til next time,

V

June 22, later

Hunter is signed up for the second session at the Gibson Prep School camp and now Pete wants to go too. Actually, it's not really a camp, not in the traditional sense. There's no pool or playground, no hiking or arts and crafts. It's more like summer school without grades or tests. There are two classes a day with an hour break for lunch. Hunter is taking a class on the Civil War, and another on the Vikings.

I called the camp but the secretary insisted that there were no openings. I offered to pay double the fee. She put me on hold, returned five minutes later, and told me that she could, in fact, make an exception, given my willingness to compensate the camp appropriately.

'Til next time,

V

June 23

I wish I could freeze this feeling forever.

It is 12:09 A.M. I have been with Michael Avila for six

utterly transcendent hours. I'm too wary to say I'm in love, but I'm definitely enchanted.

Even with all my new clothes, I couldn't find anything formal enough for the ballet. I finally settled on a long black skirt, cream-colored embroidered top, short black velvet jacket. Michael looked sleek and delicious in a jet-black tux.

Michael gave me a bouquet of pastel roses, Asiatic lilies, and alstroemeria, and when I went to hug him, he kissed me on the cheek and it felt soft and warm. He told me that I looked even prettier with short hair, that it brought out the green in my eyes. I *felt* pretty under his gaze. I felt tall and slim and attractive and special and sparkly.

I think he was expecting to meet Pete, but I'd arranged for Pete to sleep at Drew Steuben's house. (Pete had begged me to let him stay with Hunter, but I'm still feeling icky about Lynette and Curtis.)

We started the evening at Bellamy's and I took it as a rather romantic choice, since this was where we had our first date, the one my mother had engineered. Though pricey, the food at Bellamy's is consistently good and is prepared by actual trained grown-ups— noteworthy in a town where most restaurants are staffed by college kids whose culinary repertoire is limited to "three minutes on full power."

Michael suggested we order two dishes to share, another happy signal. Roger *hated* sharing food. He thought it was unhygienic. We started with a bottle of

Möet Et Chandon and appetizers: sauteed almonds and marinated roasted olives (yum!), then moved to the chicken fricassee with ginger, scallions, sweet peppers, onions, and shiitake mushrooms (sublime), and gnocchi with wild mushrooms, truffles, and scallions (perfect). For dessert, one crème brûlée, two spoons (his choice, above my protestations that I needed to watch my weight).

By 8 P.M. we were settled into our plum-colored velvet seats at the Performing Arts Center. *Appalachian Suite,* I learned from the program, focuses on a younger pioneer couple in early-nineteenth-century Pennsylvania. Composed by Aaron Copland for Martha Graham, the music was strong and optimistic. The program included a quote from Martha Graham, who wrote that the *Appalachian Suite* "is essentially the coming of new life. It has to do with growing things." She said that spring was the loveliest but also the saddest time. I thought about the coming of my new life, the growing of a new relationship. I was enchanted by the loveliness of this moment with Michael, but I was also sad. Was I grieving for what I'd lost? Or because I suspected that happiness would always elude me, that even this budding relationship was doomed?

I suggested Starbucks after the ballet; I didn't want to leave him. I noticed that women seemed drawn to him—the counter girl at Starbucks actually gave him a plate of lemon tarts for free. I also noticed that Michael didn't eye anyone, not even the striking girl in the slim black skirt and stiletto sandals, or the Polynesian-looking beauty working on a laptop at the table next to ours. Nor did he flirt back when the counter girl said she was sizzling hot and wished she could go skinny-dipping. More happy signals!

I told him about Jerry Johansen and he listened intently ("with both ears and both eyes," as Pete's teacher likes to say).

There was one more uncomfortable topic I'd wanted to get out of the way. "I think we have a mutual friend," I started.

"Really? Who?" Michael asked.

"Diana Pierce."

He looked at me blankly.

"Dark hair? Slim? Pretty?" I continued.

Michael shrugged. "Sorry. Don't know her." He looked into my empty cup. "I'm getting a refill. Want one?"

"No thanks," I told him. I watched him walk back to the counter and admired his firm round buns.

After coffee, Michael invited me to see his new house, but—remembering commandment number four—I politely declined. He frowned. "You sure?" he asked, picking a bit of fuzz off my jacket.

I hesitated, then smiled. "I'm sure. Maybe next time," I said, amazed by my self-restraint.

He drove me home and walked me to the porch, then gave me a long hug. He kissed me first on the cheek, then lightly on the lips. I had to stand on my toes to reach him. He said he'd call me soon, mentioned something about football tickets. I was elated, and to hell with the ten commandments of dating. I wanted to ask him inside. Instead, I watched him walk back to his car. He waved as he pulled away from the curb.

I know I should go to sleep now but I think I'll just sit here and feel this quiet joy.

'Til next time,

V

June 27

Nancy Cooperman says that at the rate I'm spending, I may be broke by the end of the year. She was being facetious, of course, but I took it as a warning. She sent me a book about millionaires, said it was an early Christmas present. The author says that many of the wealthiest people in America live most modestly. They drive older model cars, shop at Sears, live in middle-class neighborhoods. They got rich by investing conservatively and spending frugally, and while this doesn't mean I have to go back to recycling bra straps, Nancy said I probably shouldn't spend $200 the next time a Girl Scout comes to the door selling peanut brittle. (But I *had* to! I felt so sorry for the little girl. She said she never sells anything and therefore never wins any of the prizes. This year, thanks to me, she's guaranteed to win the Barbie sleeping bag!)

I'd like to be the kind of millionaire that lives modestly . . . someday. But first I'm reveling in my wealth. I can buy any damn thing I want and nobody's going to stop me. I'm going to replace the white tile in my kitchen (aka the dirt magnet) with Mediterranean-style tile that looks rustic and dirty already and hides everything. But the smaller luxuries are the ones that really thrill me: A Gore-Tex winter cap. Vanity Fair dinner napkins. A twelve-pack of mechanical pencils. A new pair of shoes (and not because I needed them).

And I love being able to give to charity. I've sent a thousand dollars to the library fund at Pete's school, another thousand to the women's shelter. I plan to talk to Nancy about setting up a endowment for the community kitchen. I *love* spending money this way!

'Til next time,

V

June 29

It's almost midnight and I've been playing Solitaire 'Til You Drop on my computer for over an hour. I'm completely addicted to this game. I've come to realize that it's a metaphor for life.

Sometimes the cards all seem to be in your favor—all

the aces fall into place, the kings line up just right—
and even then you wind up losing because there's a
glitch, some critical card isn't dealt and you're stuck.
Other times it looks like you've been dealt a losing
hand, but you play it anyway and suddenly, against all
expectations and odds, you've won the game.

After playing for years, I've only recently discovered
that you can undo all your moves right up to the first
one. If only life were that easy.

I've decided to call C.J. Patterson. I'm not done with
Jerry Johansen yet.

'Til next time,

V

July 2

The phone rang at 8 A.M. I roused myself, frantically
tried to clear my throat, did not want to sound like a
braying donkey in case it was Michael calling. It wasn't.

"So how was your date with hunky Detective Avila?"

"Diana. It's eight in the morning. On Sunday.
Shouldn't you be asleep?"

"Oh, baby, did I wake you? So sorry! You know how
it is with us early birds. By eight o'clock I'm ready for
lunch."

"Can I go back to sleep now?"

"Not until you tell me how your date went. Was it
everything you'd dreamed it would be?"

This line of questioning made me uneasy. I knew that Diana couldn't possibly be rooting for Michael and me. I decided that the less I told her, the better. "It was fine, Diana."

"Fine. Be that way," she said. "That's not why I called. I've got news about Roger."

Now I was wide awake. "Tell me."

"He's out of jail. He's living with his little girlfriend and her parents. And he wants to see Pete."

"Over my dead body."

"You know, according to your temporary custody agreement, he's allowed to see Pete. You can't keep him from his son."

"Oh? And now you're defending that jackass?"

"No, not defending. Just telling the truth. If you make trouble now, it could work against you later, when you finalize the agreement. You get one of those fathers'-rights type judges and you could lose Pete altogether. I'd hate to see that happen to you."

"I'd never lose Pete," I said, trying to sound confident as I felt tremors right down my spine. "That can't happen."

"Look, if he wants to see Pete, let him. That's all I'm saying." And then, as if on cue, there was a knock on the door.

"Did you send him over here?" I asked Diana.

"Who? Roger? No!" she said.

"I think he's at the door," I said.

"Don't answer it. Just ignore it."

The knocking continued, louder now. I ran into the guest room and peered between the blinds. I couldn't see Roger but I spotted his Lexus SUV at the curb. I ran back to the phone. "I've got to go," I told Diana.

"Be strong, baby," she said. "Don't let him in."

"Not by the hair of my chinny chin chin," I said, and hung up the phone. I pulled my gray sweatpants off the Nordic Trak and checked my face in the mirror. I wiped the old mascara off my face, swished and spat a capful of Listerine, and stumbled down the steps. I swung open the front door, but kept the glass storm door closed and locked. Roger stood with his arms crossed tightly against his chest. He was wearing a tailored shirt, new black jeans, and new sneakers. (Where was he getting the money to buy new clothes?) His pale blond hair was cropped so closely it looked as if someone had spray-painted his skull. He wore a tiny gold hoop in his right ear. He seemed to be growing a beard.

He slid his sunglasses down his nose. "Nice hair," he said, smirking. He put his hand on the storm door handle. "I want to see Pete."

"Pete's sleeping," I told him. I had no intention of telling him that Pete was sleeping at Drew's. I didn't want him harassing the Steubens.

"I want to see him now." He jiggled the handle impatiently. I looked toward his SUV and noticed Surfer Girl in the passenger seat. The mirror was flipped down. She was slicking her lips with gloss. She must have sensed that I was watching her because she swiveled her head toward me and smiled.

"You can't see him now, Roger. He's sleeping."

Roger glanced at his watch. "Wake him up. He's had enough sleep. I want to see him." He jiggled the door again. "Open the damn door. I have a right to see my son." He stepped back off the porch and looked up toward Pete's window. "Petey Boy! Pete! Peeetttterrrr!" He was bellowing now. "Wake up, Pete! It's Daddy! Wake up, honey!"

"Give it up, Roger. He's not coming down."

Roger shot me a malignant glare. "I have the right to see my son."

"No you don't. Right now I've got full custody. You know that."

"I don't care what the papers say. Pete is my son and I want to see him."

I glanced toward the SUV. Surfer Girl was pulling a comb through her flowing blond hair. "Go away, Roger," I told him. "Go take your girlfriend to Chuck E. Cheese's." I closed the door slowly, deliberately. I locked it and watched through the window as Roger stood there, staring up at Pete's window. Finally, he gave up. At least for the moment.

'Til next time,

♍

July 3

Michael hasn't called, but Lynette has. She left a message on my machine. She wants to meet for lunch. I haven't called her back.

'Til next time,

V

July 4

I saw Lynette at the bus stop this morning. Her hair was pulled back in a neat ponytail and she was wearing pale lipstick, a hint of blush, no mascara. I, on the other hand, was wearing the same sweats I'd slept in, a pajama top without a bra, and slippers. Whatever makeup I'd had on my face was left over from last night.

"You didn't return my call," she said as the bus heaved and rattled down the street. I pretended to wave at Pete. In fact, the windows were tinted and I couldn't make out anyone's face, let alone Pete's.

"I'm sorry, Lynette. I've been so busy."

"Oh, I understand." She began to turn away.

"Wait. Lynette. I'm lying."

She turned toward me and waited.

"It's just that, I feel so, I don't know . . ."

"Weird?"

"Weird's a good word," I said.

"I feel weird too," she said. "It was a weird night. But

I never thought you'd stop talking to me because of it. I guess I thought you'd be more understanding." She looked down at the ground and paused for a moment. "It's not like you've never veered off the straight and narrow. No offense."

She was right, of course. But I couldn't expunge the image of Lynette and Curtis and Wade and Melanie contorting themselves on Lynette's queen-size bed, atop the blue and yellow Amish quilt that Lynette's mother had given them for their tenth wedding anniversary. Why couldn't I just ease up and be her friend again? "No offense taken," I said, trying to stoke the remaining embers of goodwill. "How's Hunter?" I asked.

"Oh, he's fine," she chirped, clearly thrilled that I was willing to talk to her. "He's lobbying for that new Play Station" She rolled her eyes. "I told him that Santa's still waiting for a thank-you note for the Nintendo." She looked at me. "And he really misses Pete."

"Maybe we can get them together over the weekend," I suggested.

"Oh, Hunter would love that!" she said. She said she was trying to get an early start on making beginning-of-the-year gifts for the teachers, and maybe Pete would like to get involved. She had an idea for filling teacups with chocolate-dipped spoons and little packs of flavored instant coffee. "It's really easy, and so yummy!" I told Lynette that I'd send Pete over on Saturday afternoon, and then maybe I could have Hunter in the evening for a sleepover.

"Really? Oh! That would be great!" She was beaming now and it made me feel guilty. I'd behaved punitively toward her, and why? Because she'd tumbled—consensually—into bed with another couple?

Exactly.

'Til next time,

V

July 5

I spent the morning online, researching prostate cancer treatments. I found an intriguing trial in Los Angeles, made a few phone calls, and managed to get my father an interview with the oncologist who is heading up the research. But when I called my mother, she had an entirely different idea.

"Forget the doctors," she told me. "Let's take your father to Medjugorje."

"You want to take him where?"

"Medjugorje. People come from all over to be healed. They see visions of the Virgin Mary."

"Mother, you're kidding, right?"

"I'm absolutely serious. I saw a TV special on this place. It's amazing. People see apparitions, they experience miraculous healings. Valerie. We've gone the medical route. I want to try it. Please."

I didn't know what to say. My mother had never really

begged me for anything. "But we're not even Catholic."

"It doesn't matter. Anyone can go. Valerie. Please. It's our last hope. Your father wants to do this."

I sighed. "Where is this place?"

"It's a village in Bosnia-Herzegovina."

"WHAT? Are you crazy? We'll get ourselves killed."

"No, no. It's fine, it's safe. We'll go with a group. We'll be fine. Please, Val. Let's do this. Let's go to Medjugorje."

"Okay, Mom." I sighed. "We'll go. We'll go to Medjugorje."

And we will.

'Til next time,

V

July 6

Went to Talbot's today for a new outfit. My mission: To dress like a Mushroomhead. I bought a pale blue crepe jacket ($184), matching slacks ($89), and strappy sandals ($110).

Now that I've got the outfit, tomorrow I'm paying a visit to C.J. Patterson. I'm going to make her an irresistible offer. And then I'm calling Omar to push for a permanent custody agreement so Roger will never, ever get his hands on my son.

'Til next time,

V

July 7

Met with C.J. She was wearing the same blue crepe suit. We tittered politely and I said something lame like "Great minds shop alike." When she went upstairs to get her reading glasses, she came down wearing a white sundress.

My plan went beautifully. I offered her $25,000 for the hospital foundation, but first she had to do me a small favor.

"I want you to press charges against Jerry Johansen."

"What?"

"You heard me. I want you to call the police and press charges."

"But he's gone. What's the difference?"

"The difference is that he's creepy, and whether he lives here or in Wyoming, he shouldn't be coaching little boys."

C.J. smoothed her highlighted hair with both hands. "Why can't you do this? Peter is involved in this too."

"Because I've got enough legal activity in my life right now. And because you're a respected member of our community. Your husband golfs with the D.A. and you play bridge with his wife. You can make it happen C.J., I don't have that kind of pull in this town."

C.J.'s cheeks reddened as she absorbed the compliment.

"I'd love to support the hospital. But it's hard for me to think about making big donations when I've got this other thing on my mind." My sandals were killing me.

"Okay. I'll have my husband make a phone call. I'm sure we can get this matter resolved. And in the meantime . . ." She flashed a slick, solicitous smile.

I pulled out my checkbook. I wrote out a check for $25,000, ripped it out, and handed it to her. "It's my pleasure to help the hospital foundation," I said. "You gals do wonderful work."

Did I just say "gals"?

'Til next time,

V

July 8

When I got back from the mall with Pete, I found a message on the machine from Michael. He wants to see me tonight. I'd like to see him, too. But Hunter is supposed to sleep here. I'd have to get a sitter. Or send them both to Lynette's house. Then again, I think it's a mistake to take every offer, especially one on such short notice. On the other hand, I'm too old to play games. I like him, he likes me, would it really hurt for me to see him tonight?

'Til next time,

V

July 8, later

Decided against going out with Michael tonight. He was disappointed but perfectly understanding. I rented *Toy Story 2* for the boys, made a giant bowl of popcorn, and snuggled with them in the family room. Michael called at 9 P.M. to say he was thinking of me and asked if we got to the part in the movie when Jessie the cowgirl sings that sweet, heartbreaking song about being outgrown by the girl who once played with her. Michael confessed that he had cried the first time he saw that scene, and I admitted that I'd sobbed so loudly I had to go sit in the bathroom until I could pull myself together. He said he was going to his parents' next Sunday and asked if I wanted to join him (whoa!), but I told him that my sisters and I would be having a little reunion at my folks' house, to relish whatever time we have left with my father. I'm thrilled Michael would consider introducing me to his family. I also wonder if he was fishing for an invitation to watch the movie with me and the boys, but I'm not about to introduce him to Pete—yet.

'Til next time,

V

July 9

My sister, Mother Teresa, insisted on cooking EVERY-THING for dinner, not because she's an altruist, but a control freak who believes that she is the only one capable of cooking an edible meal. I'm sure that my other sister, Julia, would have been delighted to let Teresa handle all the cooking, and I probably would have acquiesced just to avoid a confrontation with my pig-headed big sister, but this time I insisted that we all pitch in. In fact, I volunteered to grill chicken, an offer I now regret because I hate standing over a flaming grill.

So I've just killed the last two hours surfing the Web for new recipes. I wanted to dig up one recipe in particular, an absolutely sublime sweet potato dish I'd found online three years ago and, naturally, never filed. I was just about to give up when miraculously I found the site with the recipe for glazed maple sweet potatoes. The last time I made it, I regretted I hadn't doubled the recipe because it was gone in a flash. Everyone was yum-yumming over the sweet potatoes, everyone except Teresa—who had three helpings, by the way. I think I'll also make cooked cranberry sauce with toasted walnuts and mandarin oranges. Easy, delicious.

As for the chicken, I'm not sure whether I want to go sweet or spicy. I've got a good recipe for lemon-oregano roasted chicken . . . but where the heck is it??? My kitchen is a mess and I've come to realize that it probably doesn't matter how rich I am, I will always be disorganized. The little telephone table off the kitchen is piled high with junk mail, bills, Pokémon cards, assorted nonfunctioning pens, Post-it notes, school notices (most of which have expired), a stray slice of American cheese and three cheese wrappers, a tiny Monopoly game key chain and unwanted Halloween candy (the kind even I won't eat).

All our plans are set for Medjugorje and I'm uncharacteristically calm about the flight. Normally I depend on a glass of wine to help me survive even the quick trip to Chicago. Now I'm flying across the world and I'm actually looking forward to it. I am on a mission and I'm too focused on my father to feel nervous about flying. If there is a God, He has to be looking out for us. This flight can't possibly be doomed.

I bought five tickets, one each for me, Dad, Mom, Pete, and my sister Teresa, who begged to come along. I agreed to let her come, if only because I'll need someone to help me carry Dad's wheelchair up Apparition Hill, where the visions of Mary are said to take place. It was too late to hook up with a group, but I found a driver as well as a guide, a priest, actually, who does nothing but help Americans make the pilgrimage to Medjugorje. I booked us rooms in the Anamaria, one of the two bigger hotels in the area. I'd wanted to rent a bungalow but the bungalow village is already full of Spanish peacekeeping forces. We're leaving two weeks from yesterday. Total cost of trip: $29,487, which includes plane fare, rooms, guides, and gas (3.80 kuna per liter. I don't know what a kuna is. Nor do I know what a liter is. I never learned the metric system. Is it a gallon? A cup?).

'Til next time,

𝒱

July 10

It's raining. I think I'm getting the flu. I want to go back to bed.

But I think I'll go shopping instead. I know I should be a bit more high-minded about this newfound wealth, but I've got to be honest: I LOVE BEING RICH! I can buy any damn thing I want and it won't even make a dent in my bank account. I bought myself the diamond ring Roger would never have bought me, a flawless two-carat rock. The truth is, I'd discouraged Roger from buying me an engagement ring. He'd made it clear that he thought they were pointless symbols of materialism and female bondage, and I pretended to agree with him. So we opted for matching mopeds and skipped the ring altogether. A year after our marriage his mother guilted him into buying me a diamond ring, but it was one of those optical illusion deals: a teeny semiprecious stone surrounded by a bunch of microscopic diamond chips and bevels. If you look really close, you can see the inscription inside the stone: your husband is a cheap asswipe.

I think I'm going to hire a personal trainer, the same woman who transformed Katie Couric's body. She charges $7,500 a week, but she'll probably want more since she'll have to camp out here in the hinterlands for a few months while she turns my blobbified body into a lean, mean, gorgeous machine. I read somewhere that this trainer—who goes by the name High Voltage—will want me to give up sugar, flour, and salt. I don't know if I'm ready for that! Especially not sugar. Or flour. Maybe salt. Maybe not.

I'm sick of my stupid washing machine. It's the low-end model Roger had insisted we buy because he didn't want to shell out the extra $200 for the better brand. The big problem is that it can't handle towels or blankets. Try to wash a beach towel and the dang thing starts buzzing in the middle of the spin cycle and you have to stand there lifting and lowering the door like a ninny until the water drains. So today I'm going to buy me the best washing machine I can find, and maybe a new dryer, too, just for the hell of it.

'Til next time,

V

July 11

Boyfriend, boyfriend, I've got a boyfriend (to be sung to the tune of "Baby, Baby, Stick Your Head in Gravy").

Michael called me again, just to check in. He said he missed me. He said he saw a dress that would go perfect with my coloring, and almost bought it for me but wasn't sure what size I wore (as if I would ever tell him?!?!). I told him about the trip to Medjugorje and he asked, only half-kiddingly, if I might like to have police protection. When I got home from picking Pete up, I found a gift bag on the porch. Inside, a book called *The Visions of the Children: The Apparitions of the Blessed Mother at Medjugorje*. Inside the bag I also found a pair of warm, nubby socks with a note attached: "You'll need these to keep those pretty tootsies warm on the hike up the hill."

What a guy.

Lynette invited Pete over to her house after school to make paper bag puppets. Much to her astonishment, I invited Hunter to our house instead, for an afternoon of crafts. I'd gone to Borders to buy a book of easy projects, then stopped at the Hobby Lobby for $203 worth of supplies. I cringed when the cashier told me my total, then I remembered: Hey, I'm rich. I can afford this. I bought everything Roger always insisted we didn't need: glue guns, a paper crimper, laminating machine, a dozen rubber stamps and ink pads in every color, unfinished wooden thingamajigs, fabric paints, glitter, markers, modeling clay you can bake in the oven, mosaic kits, fake flower garlands, candy molds, Styrofoam topiary shapes, two big bags of assorted buttons, and pipe cleaners—which, someone has apparently decided, must now be called chenille craft sticks.

So I told Lynette to send Hunter over. We made bird feeders, chocolate suckers, apple votive holders, and gumdrop sculptures. I wish I could have seen Lynette's face when Hunter walked in with his handmade bounty.

I spent the rest of the day preparing for the trip to Medjugorje and I'm starting to get nervous. I don't know how I'm going to navigate our family through this foreign land for two weeks. We don't speak Croatian. What if our guide doesn't show up? What if our driver is a drunken lunatic? What if another war breaks out? What if Teresa and I can't carry the wheelchair up the hill?

We'll need waterproof jackets in the event it rains while we're climbing Mt. Podbrdo (Apparition Hill), and we'll need sturdy shoes to make it up the rocky terrain. It takes ten to fifteen minutes to get up the hill, but I suspect it takes longer when you're dragging up a wheelchair. We'll also need to pack flashlights, because there's no street lighting in parts of Medjugorje.

'Til next time,

𝒱

July 12

Roger has crossed the line this time.

At 2:56 P.M. I got a call from the secretary at Pete's

camp. "Mrs. Tisdale, this is Roberta Burns," she started.

"Is Pete okay?"

"Well, he's fine, but we have a *situation.*"

"What is it?" My mind flooded with possibilities. Had he pooped in his pants? Had he whacked another kid with a stick?

"Your husband is standing here now. He says he's here to pick up Peter."

Good God. "Please, Roberta, don't let him take Pete anywhere. He has no right to take my son."

"He insists that he is well within his rights. And the camp has no power to stop him."

I told her to hang up and that I'd call right back on my cell phone. "Keep Pete in his room. I'll be there in four minutes," I said as I ran to my Jeep.

"I don't know that I can do that," Roberta whispered. "Mr. Tisdale insists he has the right to take Peter home with him."

"He doesn't have custody. I do."

"I don't understand. You're divorced?"

"Yes. We're divorced."

"But our records indicate that you're married. It says right here. Camper resides with both parents at—"

"Forget that," I interrupted. "I never updated Pete's files. My mistake. I've been busy."

"I see." The two words projected volumes about my negligence, my disorganization, my incompetence. How could anyone blame me for failing to fill out yet another form? I was floundering in a flood of notices. Every day Pete's backpack was stuffed with fliers. There were fliers about Family Camping Day. International Festival Day. Science Exploration Day. Camper Appreciation Day. Field trip permission slips. Permission slip so camp may post child's artwork. Permission slip so child may use the Internet. Permission slip so child may be photographed for camp Web page. Canned food drive. The electric fans for the hot poor people drive. Jump-Rope-a-Thon for Multiple Sclerosis. Penny drive for United Way. Fund-raising appeals for new playground equipment, new gardens, new carpeting in the cafeteria.

It never ended!

I had to get through to the camp director. "Let me talk to Mr. Enright, please."

"He's on another line."

"Oh come on, Roberta. He's right next door. This is an emergency. Get him off the other line."

"Yes, of course."

"This is Mr. Enright," the camp director intoned, sounding uncannily like Al Gore. "Can I help you?" He acted as if he was unaware of the crisis that was now unfolding two feet outside his office.

"Look. My husband is standing at Roberta's desk right now. He's demanding to pick up my son, Mr. Enright. You can't let him take him. My husband is unstable. He doesn't have custody."

"I understand, Mrs. Tisdale."

"It's not Mrs. Tisdale. It's Ms. Ryan. We're divorced. Please. Listen to me. You can't let Roger take my son."

"He says he's well within his rights."

"He's wrong. And let me make myself clear. If my husband leaves that building with my son, you'll have a lawsuit on your hands that'll make your head spin."

"I understand. I do." I heard the principal call out to Roberta. "I'm going to get security over here now. Your son is safe here. We'll keep him upstairs with his teacher. They'll keep the doors locked. They know the drill. This isn't the first time we've been caught in a custody crossfire."

Custody crossfire? The phrase made me sick. Pete was trapped between rocks and rubber bullets like some bewildered American tourist on the Gaza Strip. We were just another rancorous divorced couple wreaking havoc in our kid's life.

As I sped through the stop sign at Atkins and Long, I saw police car lights spinning behind me. I decided to let the cop trail me into the parking lot. I pulled up to the curb in front of the school, hopped out of the Jeep, and rushed to the police car. "I know I was speeding. I'm sorry. You can give me a ticket later. I'm not a fugitive. I'm just a mother. Please. You've got to help me. My husband is trying to kidnap my son!"

The officer, a kindly-looking man who must have been nearing retirement, looked sincerely concerned. "Don't worry about the ticket, darlin'." He had his hand on his gun. He brought his radio to his mouth and called for backup. This was working out splendidly.

The office was packed with bodies: Robert, Mr. Enright, Roger, the burly lifeguard and the deaf one-armed custodian, both of whom double as the camp's unofficial security guards. The small office reeked of sweat and potpourri and Charlie (Roberta's favorite perfume, apparently). Roger was wearing the same getup he'd worn to my house the other day, with one new addition, a black beret. He held an unlit cigarette between his fingers. Surfer Girl was there too.

Roger sneered at me. "You can't keep him from me." He cocked his head toward the police officer. "What's with Officer Friday?"

"It's Officer Navansky," the cop said. "And you're not going anywhere until you can prove custodial rights over your child."

The dismissal bell chimed and the main corridor to the exit was teeming with kids hobbling under the weight of their backpacks. They gawked at the windows. I heard one say, "That's Pete Tisdale's mom."

I could hear a distant chorus of sirens grow louder as they neared the camp. Soon we were joined by two more officers, a pimply kid with a bad haircut and a fetching blond who looked so good in her uniform that she must have custom-tailored the pants, a fact that didn't escape Roger's attention, even in the midst of the crisis. I watched him eye her ass. Surfer Girl saw it too and elbowed him sharply.

"We have a situation here," Officer Navansky began.

"There's no situation. I'm here to see my son. That's not a crime, is it?"

"Well, sir, it is if you don't have custody of the child."

"He doesn't, Officer," I cut in. "I have sole temporary custody."

"Roger has as much right to be with his son as you do!" Surfer Girl blurted out.

"Who's this?" Officer Navansky asked Roger.

"Not that I'm required to tell you, but the young lady is my friend."

Surfer Girl scowled at Roger. "I'm his girlfriend, Officer."

The cop shot me a sympathetic look. "I'm going to have to insist that the young lady wait outside."

She tightened her grip on Roger's arm. "I'd like to stay with my boyfriend, please. He needs the moral support."

The cop put a hand on her arm. "I'm sorry, miss. There's enough tempers flaring in this room as it is. Please wait outside."

She released her grip and reluctantly skulked out. Officer Navansky guided her with a hand on her back and closed the door behind her.

"Mr. Tisdale, is it true that your wife has sole custody of your son?"

"Temporary custody." Roger flicked an imaginary lintball off his sleeve.

"Temporary or not, is it true, sir?" Navansky pressed. "You might as well be honest, sir. One phone call and I can find out for myself."

"Yes. It's true." He stared at me acidly. I stared back.

"Then I'm going to have to ask you to remove yourself and your friend there from the premises." Officer Navansky reached for Roger's elbow. He jerked back and flailed an arm. The other cops put their hands on their guns and moved in toward Roger. Officer Navansky withdrew his hands. "You can go of your own accord, sir, or we can help you. It's your choice."

Roger straightened his beret and shot me another corrosive stare. "Keep your hands off me. I'm going."

"You can give me that ticket now if you want to," I told Officer Navansky, aware of the guile in my suggestion. I knew he wouldn't ticket me.

"No, no, just forget about it." He put a fatherly arm around my shoulder. "My own daughter has the same problem with her ex. That creep left her for a younger gal and now he thinks he has the right to see his kid whenever he pleases. Let me tell you, I would have killed the son of a bitch myself if I didn't think I'd lose my pension."

'Til next time,

V

July 16

I'm glad my family's little reunion is over. What an emotionally draining day, and not only because my father is dying, but because I could see how my mother has neglected her home (I found mouse droppings in the kitchen drawers) and, because Teresa managed to eat every perfect dish I served without a single word of praise, and because Julia yet again made separate meals for her spoiled twins yet never once asked how Pete and I are holding up since the divorce, and because Roger called in the middle of dinner to say hi to Pete and Surfer Girl was on the line and told Pete that she can't wait to give him a little present, and because we're leaving for Bosnia-Herzegovina in a week and I'm beginning to fear that our plane is going to nosedive into the sea. Of all the ways to die, that's got to be the worst. Now my stomach hurts. I've got to go to the bathroom.

I'm back.

The best thing about dinner was that everything I made was delicious, even if Teresa wasn't big enough to admit it. The derby pie (Pete's favorite) was obscenely wonderful. I've decided to put the recipe down in this journal so I can't possibly lose it.

Derby Pie, also known as heart attack in a pie shell

1 stick melted butter
1 cup sugar
2 eggs, lightly beaten
½ cup flour
1 teaspoon vanilla
1 cup chocolate chips
1 cup pecans (I skipped the pecans since Pete hates nuts.)

Combine all ingredients and pour into frozen pie shell. Bake at 325 degrees for 1 hour. (I baked it for an extra fifteen minutes, then chilled it outside on the deck. It's supposed to be sort of runny.)

The other hit was my personal favorite:

Glazed maple sweet potatoes, also known as adult onset diabetes in a Corning casserole dish.

10 sweet potatoes, cooked, peeled, and sliced
1 cup maple syrup
3 tablespoons butter
½ cup apple cider
1 teaspoon salt
4 tablespoons maple sugar (I used brown sugar.)

Preheat oven to 300 degrees. Place sweet potatoes in greased casserole dish. In separate pot mix up syrup, butter, cider, brown or maple sugar, and salt and bring to boil. Pour mixture over potatoes. Bake 45 minutes, basting every 15 minutes.

'Til next time,

V

July 17

I called Omar to let him know about the trip to Medjugorje so he could schedule the custody hearing accordingly. He was out of the office, so I left a message. I hate waiting so long to finalize my custody arrangement, but I don't see that I have a choice now. I only hope that Roger doesn't try to abduct Pete.

I did something uncharacteristically spontaneous today. I called my new friend Donna Gold and invited her and her family for take-out dinner. Donna was as buoyant as ever, but her husband wasn't at all what I'd expected from my elegant Southern friend. Christopher was quiet, bespectacled, and balding. They made such an unlikely pair that I decided it he must be hung like a donkey and fabulous in bed. After dinner, Christopher took all the kids to play putt-putt, "To give you ladies a chance to talk," he said, winking.

"Don't believe it for a minute," Donna said, tossing a crumpled paper napkin at her husband. "Christopher's just a big ole kid. He just wants to play putt-putt and he's using our kids as a cover."

"Okay, okay, you got me," he said, throwing up his arms in surrender.

After they left, Donna and I cleaned up the kitchen and talked. I gave her an only slightly sanitized version of my marriage, and she confessed that she'd had her share of problems with Christopher, but survived with the help of an "amazing" therapist (Bonita Loeb, as it turned out. I decided not to tell her that Roger and I were Bonita Loeb rejects). She didn't detail her marital problems, and I didn't probe, but I expect I'll find out eventually.

I told Donna about Roger's latest antics. "At least I'll have permanent custody before too long," I said.

She shook her head. "How can you be so sure?" she asked.

"Come on. What judge is going to give that bastard custody of Pete? After everything Roger has done?"

"Well, maybe not full custody, but the judge might give him joint custody." Donna saw the incredulity on my face. "Hey, it happens. Especially these days. Fathers' rights, you know." She told me about Tamara Parker, a mother in her play group. "Her ex-husband was the worst." She paused. "Okay, maybe not the worst, but he ran a close second to your beaut. He knocked up their baby-sitter. And he left her practically destitute. Now he's got joint custody of the kids. Him and his new wife. The baby-sitter."

I told her I didn't want to talk about it. "Let's talk about something nice instead."

I told her about Michael Avila. "When I'm with him I just feel so cared for, so safe, so listened to," I said. "But . . ."

"What is it?"

I told Donna something I hadn't yet admitted to myself. "No big fireworks, I guess. You know. There's something missing. The chemistry. At least for me."

"Not nasty enough for ya, huh?"

"What?"

"Let's see. He's not a cheater, he's not a liar, he doesn't have another wife hidden in a condo somewhere, he doesn't have a yen for teenagers . . . no wonder you're not attracted to him!" Donna put her hands on her hips and stared at me. "Listen to me, girl, and listen good. If this detective of yours is as sweet and kind and good-looking as you say he is, you'd be a fool to let him go just because he doesn't get you all hot and bothered. In my humble opinion"—she shoved the gravy boat into the dishwasher—"I think you need to rejig your definition of sexy."

Maybe I do. But how?

'Til next time,

V

July 21

My mother told me that over the last few months Dad has been seeking the Divine, "like a wilting flower thirsting for rainwater," is how she put it. He reads the Bible and watches the TV preachers, and even called once and asked their "prayer buddies" to pray with him, to pray for him. I interpreted this more as an act of desperation than true religious conversion, but I wasn't about to tell my mother that.

She has been researching Medjugorje. Apparently, there are special prayers for healing the sick, and these must each be recited seven times: The Creed, The Lord's Prayer, the Hail Mary, and Glory Be. (I know the Lord's Prayer, but as for the rest, I'm clueless. My mother has printed them out for each of us but my father already has them memorized.) He will need to fast on bread and water, and when we meet up with our priest, my father will be anointed with some kind of holy oil. Supposedly it's critical to get the right priest for the job because not all have the "gift of healing." They say that only priests who pray with forbearance and firm belief will have God's ear. I only hope that's the kind I've hired.

I'm still incredulous, but I'm beginning to feel inspired. Maybe there really is hope for my father.

'Til next time,

V

July 22

At 5 A.M. I roused Pete and we took a cab to my mother's house. I asked the driver to wait outside. "We'll be just a minute," I told him.

"No problem. Take your time. I've got my breakfast here," he said, pulling an Egg McMuffin out of a McDonald's bag. I had no appetite.

My mother met me on the porch. She was wearing her coat and gloves. "Your father isn't doing very well."

I stepped over the two small suitcases at the door. Pete scrambled down to the basement to explore my father's old armoire. It was filled with pads and markers and assorted office supplies, playing cards and books about the Korean War. He could spend all day down there and never come up for a snack.

My father was sitting on the couch, laboring to breathe. His stocking feet looked so small and frail. He managed a smile. "Valerie," he whispered.

"It all happened so suddenly," my mother said, her hands fluttering like moths. "He was up and about yesterday.

"It's time to go, Dad," I told him. "The driver's waiting outside." My father sat passively as I gently pulled on his hat and wrapped the scarf around his neck. I could feel his sharp shoulder blades through his baggy beige fisherman's sweater. His skin was translucent and his eyes were an entirely new color, not the green I'd remembered but the softest blue-gray, the color of the summer sky at dawn. Even as I buttoned up his jacket, I knew we weren't going anywhere.

"Tell me about the Blessed Virgin," he said. "Tell me about miracles. His voice was wispy as smoke. His mouth sagged open and he gasped for air like a fish in a bucket.

I put his cold, bony hand in mine. His eyes were closed. I glanced at the driver through the picture window. He pointed to his wristwatch and raised his eyebrows.

"Mom, tell the cabdriver he can leave." I reached into my bag and grabbed a twenty. "Just give him this."

"What are you talking about?" my mother demanded. "You can't send the driver away! We need him! We've got to get to the airport!"

"Let him leave, Mom. We won't be going to the airport. We're not going anywhere."

"But Teresa. We have to meet Teresa at the airport. Get his shoes on and let's get out of here."

My father gripped my hand. "You were a beautiful baby," he said, gasping, and I felt a great sadness roll up into my throat. I didn't want to cry. My mother stood immobilized in the corner of the room, her knuckle between her teeth.

"I don't know why you made me send the driver away, Val, I really don't. We're going to miss the plane."

"My sweet Valerie, the best baby, the sweetest one." My father opened his eyes. "How is Peter?"

"I'm calling the doctor," my mother said.

"Peter's good, Dad. He's in the basement. You know how he loves to scrounge around in your old junk.

"He's a fine young man." I pulled a tissue from my sleeve and wiped the drool from my father's chin.

"Valerie," my father gasped. "Give him. My camera." My father was an amateur photographer. All my favorite photographs were the ones he captured with his Leica.

He looked directly into my eyes. He smiled.

Something had shifted.

"Where's Jack? I need Jack."

"Who's Jack, Daddy?"

"Oh!" My mother let out an anguished cry. "Jack was his dog. When he was a just a child."

"Here, Jack. Here, boy."

I wrapped my arms around my father's narrow shoulders and put my head on his chest. "Jack's right here, Daddy. He's here."

"Good Jack," my father whispered.

My mother looked horrified. I motioned for her to come over. "I love you, Daddy. We all love you so much, Daddy."

My mother knelt by my father's side. "Don't go. You can't leave me now."

"Tell him you love him," I whispered to my mother.

She sobbed loudly, gagging now. "No. I don't want to. I can't let him go."

"Tell him you love him."

My mother became very still. "I love you," she

sobbed into my father's chest. "I will always love you."

You know how they say that when you're just about to die, your whole life passes before your eyes? There must be some corollary for the person who sits with someone passing into death, for in the flicker that was my father's last breath, my life with him streamed through me. Camping at Sleeping Bear Dunes. Being hoisted high on his shoulders so I can get a better view of Cinderella in the Disney parade. Fishing with string and paper clips on the dock at Webster Lake.

And I see him buying me a purple balloon at the fourth of July parade. My father is on his knees, struggling to tie the string to my wrist. He loses the end of the string and the balloon instantly flies up. We both watch it float higher and higher into the fresh, blue, cloudless sky.

By 5:25 A.M. my father was dead.

I don't have the energy to write any more. I've got to go.

I'm back.

My father, it turns out, insisted on a traditional Irish wake. "You've got to be kidding," I told my mother. We never celebrated St. Patrick's Day. I never even had one of those "Kiss Me, I'm Irish" buttons.

"I'm serious," my mother said. She was already in Action Mode. "Your father was very clear about it. He said that when he died, I should call his great-aunt Fi-

nola and great-uncle Tim and they would handle everything."

I'd never even heard of a great-aunt Finola and uncle
Tim. As I would soon discover, there is quite a bit about
my father's family I never knew.

"The number for great-aunt Finola is on the board by
the phone," my mother continued. "Then call Rich-
mond Funeral Home and tell them your father has died
and we're having a wake. Do you have your cell
phone?"

"Yes," I told her.

"Good. Call the airport. Have Teresa paged before
she gets on that plane. I'll call Julia." She glanced
around the room and shook her head. "This place is a
mess," she said, as if she was seeing the house for the
first time. "We've got to straighten up." I was amazed
to see my mother so animated, so in control. I realize
now that a great black gloom had finally lifted. My father's death had flipped a switch. She was infused with
life now.

She asked me to help carry my father's body into the
guest room. "I can't do this," I told her. "This doesn't
seem right, dragging Dad around like a sack of laundry."

"We have to do this, Valerie."

I could have wilted and surrendered to my sorrow.
This moment was so profoundly awful. I wanted to lay
my father's body to rest, not haul him around from

room to room. For a moment I wished I were still married. This was the sort of situation I could depend on Roger to handle. At fidelity, Roger was incompetent. But when it came to killing big bugs, investigating thumps in the night, and handling other assorted domestic atrocities, Roger was supremely capable.

I stared at my father's body and somehow found the necessary detachment to grip his lifeless arms while my mother lifted his legs. I had expected him to be as light as a bag of feathers but there was a stiffness and density now that made his body feel wooden and heavy. I left my mother to arrange him while I retreated to the kitchen to call this Finola person, who didn't seem terribly shocked or saddened to learn that her nephew had died. She said she was on her way and that we should expect someone to help with the wake. I wasn't sure what she meant, and didn't ask her to elaborate. I just wanted to get off the phone.

"Are you sure Dad wanted a wake?" I asked my mother. I was still incredulous.

My mother pulled open the kitchen cabinet, the one where my parents had kept their important papers, passports, their credit cards wrapped in rubber bands, a cookie jar of cash. "It's all in here." She handed me a white envelope. "Funeral Arrangements" was written in my father's handwriting.

I opened the envelope and pulled out a sheet of yellow legal paper. "When I pass," he had written, "please contact my great-aunt Finola and great-uncle Timothy

in Boston. They will make all the necessary arrangements for a traditional Irish wake." My father had also
written his own epitaph, and my heart ached to imagine how that must have felt for him, to contemplate
and even plan his own gravestone.

"Earth has no sorrow that heaven cannot heal."

The doorbell rang at 11 A.M. I peeked out the little
window in the door. There were two women and a man
dressed in black. None looked familiar. I opened the
door. "Can I help you?"

One of the women stepped forward. "Finola Ryan
sent us. We're with the Irish American Fellowship and
we're here to help with the wake." She was beefy and
strong-looking, an inch taller than me, her long gray
hair pulled and twisted into a big bun. The other
woman was younger and equally sturdy, and there was
a tall boy, barely out of his teens, with flaming red hair.
Their clothes were worn but clean; the boy's trousers
were crisply pressed and the women seemed to have
taken great care in arranging their hair.

"I'm Rosemary O'Hara. This is Mrs. Feeney, and this
is Mr. Kilpatrick," the woman said, gesturing toward
her companions. Each regarded me with a polite nod
and I noticed that they were carrying small satchels.
"I'm sorry for your loss, ma'am," the young man said.
"Terribly sorry," Mrs. Feeney murmured. By then my
mother had joined me at the door. "I am sorry for your
loss, Missus," Mrs. O'Hara said. She extended a hand.
"Where is your husband, dear?"

My mother motioned toward the guest room, and asked, "Can I get you some coffee? Or tea?"

"No thank you, Mrs. Ryan. We're fine. Just point us in the direction of your powder room so we can wash our hands." As she spoke, she reached for the cuckoo clock on the wall and removed the battery. "We stop the clocks as a sign of respect," she said.

"The bathroom is down the hall, first door on the left," my mother directed.

Rosemary and the others hustled authoritatively down the corridor. "You are welcome to be part of this," she called out, "even if it's all new to you. It's a very special time, you know, preparing our loved ones for the hereafter."

My mother took the cordless phone to the basement to begin notifying family and friends. I stood transfixed as these three members of the Irish American Fellowship did their work. They carefully undressed my father's dead body and washed it, dipping a white washcloth into a small white porcelain basin of water. The young Mr. Kilpatrick used a blue disposable razor to expertly shave my father's face while the women quickly cleaned the room using supplies they had brought in their satchels. They lit candles on the nightstand beside the bed, then they dressed my father in a kind of religious habit, put a crucifix on his breast, and gingerly positioned a string of rosary beads in his hands. By the time they were done with him, he looked like a bishop. He no longer resembled my father. Mrs.

O'Hara saw me staring and said, "His Uncle Timothy will recite the rosary at midnight, and again in the morning."

I didn't know what to say. I felt as if our house had been conquered by guerrillas.

"I'll need several sheets," Mrs. O'Hara told me, blowing a damp tendril of curly hair off her face. "As many as you've got mirrors. Preferably white, but any will do." I was prepared to offer to buy new ones at Walmart; I didn't think my mother had kept up with the laundry. But I found a stack of clean white and pale yellow sheets in the linen closet and handed them to Mrs. O'Hara. Some of these were hung over the sides of the bed. Others were draped over mirrors.

Mrs. Feeney set a plate of something brown and dried on the dining room table. I found out later that this was snuff.

The doorbell rang and Mrs. O'Hara looked at her watch. It was 2:30 P.M. "And so it begins," she said, smiling. "Visitation will last until midnight. Someone must stay with your father at all times. One of us can spell you if you or your mother needs a break."

By six the house was filled with family and friends, a whole generation of Boston Ryans I'd never met, including the notorious Aunt Finola and Uncle Tim. She was thin and tight and humorless. He was her opposite in every way, fat and sloppy and gregarious. At one point, two grown men I'd never seen before were wrestling on the floor of the living room. Tim explained that it was a traditional "wake game." I heard my mother ask them to "play downstairs, please." I knew she didn't think it was appropriate for grown men to play games at such a somber occasion. Finola stepped forward, scowling. "It's traditional to play games at a wake," she said, and then she seemed to pull back in preparation for a strike, the way you pull an arrow back in the bow before letting it fly. "If you couldn't let your husband lead a good Irish life while he was alive, at least let him have it in death," she said sharply. "He's back in the fold now, and there's nothing you can do about it."

The room was suddenly silent as my mother seemed to shrink into herself. She bowed her head and retreated to the kitchen. My sisters and I rushed in after her. I turned around to glare at Finola, but she was laughing with another relative, apparently oblivious to the pain her tongue-lashing had caused my mother. I vaguely knew that my father had been estranged from his parents and sister since the day he announced that he would marry my mother. She wasn't Irish. She wasn't religious. In fact, she wasn't much of anything, except a pariah. Today I learned that there was an outright campaign to end my parents' engagement. The effort was led by Finola herself. And when Dad's father died of a heart attack, Finola tormented my father for months, insisting that it was my father who killed him by choosing my mother for his bride.

My mother pulled herself together and went back to

mingle among her guests. It was strange to see her so lively and, actually, happy. But why wouldn't she be? My father was at rest, and the house was filled with life, with food and flowers, with family and good friends, neighbors. And she was the center of attention. For a moment, she could forget that her husband and life companion, her best friend and soul mate, was gone forever. Eventually, the house will be empty again, the flowers will have wilted, the food will be eaten, and she will be alone. She is still relatively attractive. I wonder if she will want to date eventually.

I don't want to think about that now.

Mom came into the kitchen. "Guess who has stopped by?"

"Who?"

"Your Detective Avila."

I should have been happier to hear this. Michael walked in with a big bottle of whiskey. I took it from him and set it with the others.

"Valerie, I'm so sorry." He hugged me and kissed me lightly on the cheek. "I'm so sorry."

I asked him to sit with me on the porch and he complied, despite the fact that the air was muggy. He looked so handsome in his dark blue suit.

"Can I ask you something?" I started.

He looked apprehensive. "Sure, I guess."

"Why haven't you married?" I blurted out.

His eyes widened in surprise. He hadn't expected the question, obviously. "Well, first I was all involved in police academy and then my job, then Mom got sick and Dad really needed me, and my brother is a good-for-nothing bum so I couldn't rely on him to help—" Michael smiled. "Too much information?"

"Not at all." At this point I felt I could ask him anything. "So, you're not gay?"

"Are you kidding? Do I seem gay to you?"

I wanted to say, If you're not gay, why haven't you tried to get me into bed yet? How come you never use your tongue when you kiss me? But just then my mother walked in. "Oh, there you are!" She winked at Michael. I don't think I've ever seen my mother wink before. "Honey, would you help me inside for a minute? I need a big strong man to help me with something."

Michael sprung to his feet. "At your service." He looked at me. "We'll continue our discussion later, okay?"

I watched Michael helping my mother in the kitchen, talking with family and friends, charming my sisters and their stodgy husbands. He really did fit right in. My sister Teresa gave me a wink and a thumbs-up sign behind his back. He was perfect.

So why wasn't I madly in love?

My father's burial was at noon the next day, and by 8 P.M. the house was finally emptied of visitors. With Finola and Tim gone, we decided to remove the sheets from the mirrors, restart all the clocks, restore the guest room.

Of course, our family gatherings wouldn't be complete without at least one unpleasant confrontation. "I hear you've already got Dad's camera," Julia said, accusingly. "Don't you have enough money to buy Pete fifty new cameras?"

"Actually, I probably have enough money to buy a camera factory, Julia, but this wasn't my idea. Dad wanted Pete to have it."

"Oh really? I find that hard to believe."

"Listen. If it were up to me, you could have the damn camera and anything else you want to take from Dad's closet, but he was very clear about this. He said he wanted Pete to have the camera. I'm sorry if that's a problem for you."

"I'll bet you are."

"What is that supposed to mean?"

"Oh, nothing." She stretched a sheet of Saran Wrap over a plate of brownies. "Miss High and Mighty," she spat out. "All of a sudden you've got all this money and you think you're the boss and it's not even your money."

"Listen. Julia. We're all really strung out now. Dad's gone, it's stressful for everyone. Please. Let's pull together, at least for Mom's sake."

"Don't play therapist with me."

I know that families can get ugly when it comes to divvying up a dead person's belongings, but I never thought that would happen in my family. I realized that Julia had a whole storehouse of resentment against me for all sorts of injustices. For being the baby in the family. For winning my father's affection. For having a relatively compliant child while her own kids have been diagnosed with ADHD.

"Whatever you say, Julia. Let me know when you're ready to talk like two adults."

But that time never came. Julia and her family packed up the van and left before dinner. I haven't heard from her since.

'Til next time,

ᎶᏉ

July 27

I just received the oddest e-mail from the neighbor behind my house. At first I wondered where he had gotten my e-mail address, and then I remembered that Lynette had put together a phone and e-mail directory for our subdivision, in the deluded hope that it would help create a sense of community. Here's what he sent me:

```
Valerie Ryan:
Your sycamore trees are planted on my
property line. You must move these trees
at once or I will have no choice but to
cut them down.
Bill Stropp
```

I can't believe this! Those trees are as tall as apartment buildings. I can't possibly move them, and it would be obscene to cut them down, especially in a subdivision where full-grown trees are as rare as all-brick homes. I don't know much about this guy. He owns a chain of tire stores. I heard that his wife left him for a Goodyear rep, moved to Arizona with the kids. Lives alone in the house. House is for sale. I immediately wrote back, in my most delicately diplomatic style:

```
Dear Bill,
Thank you for expressing your concerns
about the trees. I hadn't realized that
they were planted on your property. I'm
so sorry about that, and I wish there
was something I could do. Since they are
too big to move, and it would be a shame
to remove them, perhaps I could pay you
for the property they occupy. How does
that sound to you?
Val
```

Then I got this response:

```
It sounds ridiculous. I want those trees
moved.
Bill Stropp
```

As if that wasn't enough excitement for the day, I got a call from Roger. I saw his name on Caller ID and decided not to pick up the phone. "Valerie. It's Roger. I'm suing for custody of Pete."

At first I found Roger's message amusing. What an arrogant twit! Did he actually believe in his stony black heart that he had even the remotest chance of gaining custody of Pete? I just had to call Omar, if only to share a laugh. I paged him and he called back right away.

"Valerie, I was going to phone you tomorrow," he said. I could hear the clatter of plates in the background, the cheery din of casual entertaining. Omar, I reminded myself, had a normal life, a wife who loved him and friends who enjoyed his company. He didn't spend the last forty-eight hours dragging dead bodies around his house, bickering with greedy siblings, struggling with distant relatives who believed you were bound for hell because you were a godless heathen. I pictured Omar in a linen shirt and khaki pants, fingers wrapped around a chilled stein of imported beer. I never met his wife but I imagined her slim and chic and gracious.

"Roger is suing you for custody," Omar said.

"Yes, Omar, I know. That's why I paged you. I thought you'd get a kick out of it." I managed a chuckle. "Can you believe this? What a joke. Right?"

Omar didn't say anything. "I mean, Judge Mendelsohn hates Roger. Judge Mendelsohn sent Roger to jail, for God's sake!"

"Judge Mendelsohn retired last week."

"What?"

"You heard me, Val. Judge Mendelsohn. The judge who hates Roger. The judge who sent Roger to jail. He retired last week."

I felt my throat constrict. "Are you sure?"

"Positive. I was at his retirement party. As a matter of fact, he and his wife are probably on a Carnival Cruise ship right now. Heading for the Mexican Riviera."

"Shit."

"Listen, I can't really talk now and we can't do anything at this hour anyway. Why don't you try to get some sleep, I'll try to make some calls, and we can talk again in the morning. Okay?"

No, not okay, I wanted to say. Why should I let you go back to your genteel party while I'm facing the possibility of losing my son? "Of course, of course," I said instead. "I'm sorry to have bothered you."

"No bother at all. Get some rest. We'll talk tomorrow." Click.

I suppose I could go online and shop 'til I drop, but suddenly I don't feel like spending money. I feel like throwing up.

'Til next time,

V

July 28

This just gets worse and worse. I talked to Omar this morning. Roger is definitely suing for custody, Judge Mendelsohn has definitely retired. Though destitute, Roger found himself a lawyer, the same one who represented him in the trial. Richard Sloan.

"He's doing it pro bono," Omar informed me.

"Why the hell would he do that?"

"I've got three theories. One, he's doing it out of the kindness of his heart—not likely. Two, he's hoping for a bonus down the road, once Roger's flush again."

"And when's that going to happen?" I asked.

"Who knows?"

"And what's theory number three, Omar?"

"Theory number three is a long shot, but I'm wondering if Richard's wife hates you."

"Jazzy Sloan? Why would she hate me? She doesn't even know me." Jazzy and I traveled in two entirely different hemispheres. She was the darling of the Junior League, the patron saint of the arts, Queen of the Mushroomheads.

"She knows about your generous donation to the hospital foundation. Maybe she's threatened by you. Maybe she's jealous. Who knows?"

"Okay. So Roger's suing for custody. He has a good lawyer working for free. Now what?"

"Let's see who replaces Judge Joseph. For now we sit tight. And we don't panic."

So that's what I'm doing. I'm sitting tight. And I'm not panicking. Yet.

'Til next time,

CV

July 29

Sent Pete to Hunter's house and dragged myself to the mall today. What a nightmare. Nordstroms was having some kind of big sale and the parking lot was jammed. People were parked illegally in the fire lane, in handicapped spots, in service lanes. Inside, the mall was clogged with overheated shoppers. I bought Pete a robot puppy and giant Lego set with something like nine thousand pieces, half of which he will lose by the end of the week.

I stopped at Eddie Bauer and who should I see but that stupid Bill Stropp. I walked in just as he yelled out, "Does anyone actually work in this damn store?" and watched as the harried young manager scurried up and apologetically explained that two employees had called in sick. "That's not my problem," Bill shot back. He held up a black jacket. "Now do me a favor and find me this in an extra-large." Bill Stropp has a wrestler's body, wide shoulders, thick neck, thick arms. For a heterosexual guy with no female at home to monitor his wardrobe choices, I thought he'd dressed surprisingly well. Steel blue silk T-shirt, clean stonewashed jeans, a black belt and black Doc Marten boots. His graying hair was cropped close, his eyes heavy-lidded and slate gray, his face rutted by a few old acne scars.

I still owe him a response to his last e-mail. I hate him.

Michael called me on my cell phone. He had tickets to tonight's basketball game and wanted to know if I'd join him. I took a rain check. I really need to be with Pete tonight. I told Michael about Roger's plan to sue for custody, and about Judge Mendelsohn retiring, which he already knew. "Let's hope you don't get Judge Willis," he said.

"What's wrong with Judge Willis?" I asked.

"He's the poster boy for the fathers' rights movement," Michael told me. "He's always getting quoted. National Fatherhood Initiative, men's movement, Malicious Mom Syndrome, that sort of thing."

"Malicious Mom Syndrome?"

"Oh, you know, a woman makes her kid wear flip-flops in the snow to prove that her ex-husband isn't paying enough child support. Or she intercepts birthday presents, then says, 'I guess your father forgot your birthday again this year.'"

It sounded horrible. Yet not entirely implausible. I wouldn't do it. But I understand the inclination.

'Til next time,

𝒱

July 30

Roger and his girlfriend left a present for Pete on the porch. I was tempted to throw it in the trash, and then I remembered the Malicious Mother Syndrome and put it on his bed instead.

July 31

I went online today and foraged for information on Judge Willis. Michael was right about him—he *is* a poster boy, for some nutty group called the National Men's Liberation Front. The NMLF website carries many helpful features, like:

- Fighting For Custody: Avoiding the Pitfalls
- Parental Alienation Syndrome: A Case for the Courts
- Growing Up Fatherless: The Risks
- Father Still Knows Best
- An End to Matriarchy: Make It Happen

There's one section devoted to poetry, like this inspiring verse:

Bitch, You Took My Boy Away
BY FLOYD L. HENDERSON

Bitch, you took my boy away
Just because you had a better lawyer.

Now I'm standing in the foyer
Reading Tom Sawyer
To myself.

Another section, snidely entitled, "A Mother's Love Is Like No Other," is filled with such news blurbs as:

Portland woman sentenced to 18 months for cocaine use during pregnancy. Father wins full custody.

Amanda Reynolds, 31, of Burbank, CA, stabs 2-year-old in the head with ice pick.

Birmingham, Alabama, woman suffocates newborn, dumps body in petting zoo.

In a long article on custodial rights, Judge Willis is quoted as saying, "Fathers are not sperm donors. They are the very foundation of a family, the most vital key to a child's successful future. The tradition of awarding custody to mothers simply because they have the reproductive equipment to bear children is simply misguided and it is a tradition that I will not indulge."

Judge Willis awarded full custody to a man convicted of raping his sister-in-law.

I hated to call Omar at home but I was hyperventilating. I was in the grip of a full-blown panic attack. I told him what I'd found online.

Omar sighed. "Valerie, Valerie. Didn't I tell you to sit tight? You shouldn't be researching this guy. You're only going to drive yourself crazy. You know that, don't you?"

I detected a paternal, if not patronizing tone in my attorney's voice. "Why shouldn't I get a head start on defending myself against Roger and this wacko judge? Am I supposed to sit back while Roger and his lawyer plot their plan of attack?"

Omar relented. "Well, we don't know for sure if Willis our judge, but if it makes you feel any better, why don't you meet me Thursday at noon and we'll do some strategizing of our own."

I didn't want to wait until Thursday. This had the urgency of an abnormal Pap smear. Waiting felt dangerous, risky. I was scared. But Omar explained that he had to be in court and had absolutely no time to meet me. "Okay, Omar, I'll see you Thursday."

'Til next time,

V

August 1

Michael called today to check on me. He's such a sweetheart. He invited me to dinner but I don't feel comfortable leaving Pete, and I'm not ready to invite him to the house while Pete's home.

'Til next time,

V

August 2

I finally found the time and stamina to respond to Bill Stropp's e-mail. I took a different approach this time.

```
Bill:
I've thought about the trees. They're
too large to move and I really don't
want to cut them down. We're so lucky to
have trees in our subdivision. Haven't
you enjoyed the shade they provide, and
the birds that build their homes in the
branches? These trees are such an impor-
tant part of our landscape. Please think
about it. Please?
Valerie
```

I debated whether or not to add that last "please." It sounded so whiny, so childish. Oh please, Mr. Bill, pretty please with sugar on top? I stared at the word for a long time. I decided to leave it in.

I got back this response:

```
Valerie:
I have thought about it. The birds are
noisy. I don't need the shade. Raking
the leaves is a major nuisance. I'm not
```

a tree hugger. Humans are as much a part
of the landscape as the trees. As far as
I'm concerned, my needs are as important
as any bird's.
Bill

I fired back:

I can't do anything about the birds but
I'd be happy to pay for the raking of
your leaves.

And he sent this:

Don't bother. As for the birds, I can
take care of them myself. It's hunting
season and I'm an excellent shot.

Arrrggghhhh!!! This man is driving me crazy!!

'Til next time,

V

August 3

I finally met with Omar today. "How's this all going
to shake out—assuming that Willis is our judge?" I
asked.

Omar grinned. "You know what they say about 'assume.'"

I wasn't in the mood for jokes. "Please, Omar, just answer the question."

Omar's expression was sober now. He set out a thermal carafe of coffee and two mugs. "Sloan isn't a father's rights lawyer. That's a good thing. But since Willis is such an activist for fathers' rights, it probably doesn't matter whether Sloan knows his stuff or not." He took a sip. "And that's not such a good thing. Of course, they'll try to impugn your character. That's standard."

I could feel the thunderclouds roiling in my skull, the prelude to a colossal migraine. And I felt such despair. I couldn't believe we were having this conversation. It was all so impossibly surreal, the idea that Roger might wind up with full custody. My mind raced ahead to nightmare scenarios. Surfer Girl insisting that Pete call her "Mommy." Watching Pete through Roger's living room window like some Peeping Tom. I forced myself to stay focused.

"Valerie, Are you absolutely sure that Pete is Roger's child?"

The question knocked the wind out of me. "What?"

"I'm sorry, Valerie. But I have to ask."

"Yes, I am quite certain that Roger is Pete's father. I'm not the pathological philanderer, remember?"

"Yes, of course I do. But if all else fails . . ."

"Failure is not an option, Omar." I started to cry. "I can't lose Pete. I'd kill myself."

Omar grabbed my wrist. "Hey. Don't you dare think that way. And don't you ever, *ever* let anyone else hear you say that. Roger and Sloan would have a field day with a comment like that. Do you understand me?"

I was sobbing now.

"Look. You wanted to do this, not me. I told you to relax and sit tight until we knew who the courts were assigning to the case. But you insisted. And so here we are, talking worse-case scenarios. But that's all we're doing, Valerie. We're talking. You've got to pull yourself together."

He slid a new box of tissues across the table. I grabbed a handful and wiped my face. My mascara was all over the place. I hadn't planned on crying today.

"At the risk of making you even more miserable," Omar began, and I braced myself. "Roger is going to sue for child support. My guess is he'll be aiming for twenty thousand a month, maybe more."

"You're kidding, right?" But I looked at Omar's face and knew he wasn't.

"The good news," Omar said, "is that you can afford it."

I guess that's true. But it didn't make me feel any better.

It's two in the morning. I can't sleep. What will Sloan say about me? That I cheated on my husband? That I

put my own clients at risk by skipping out of work?
That I tried to break into my supervisor's e-mail account? That I left my home every day to work downtown while my husband stayed home with Pete? It's all
true. But it hardly compares with Roger's history.

Unless we get Judge Willis.

'Til next time,

V

August 7

I fell today. Flat on my ass. Slipped on a piece of cracked
sidewalk. As I flew through the air, I had the following
train of thought: I'm slipping because my neighbors refuse to fix their sidewalk. I really should complain to
them. I could even sue them. But I haven't fixed the
cracks in my walk either. Which means that people
could just as easily slip in front of my house. And if they
do, and if they know about my divorce settlement (and
it appears that everyone in town does), they might sue
me. So I'd better start repairing my sidewalk. I'd better
go to Walmart and buy some concrete mix.

Who should I see at Walmart but Mr. Bill Stropp
himself, the lunatic, the tree hater, the maniac who lives
behind my house. He was in the hunting goods department (big surprise), and I watched as he picked out
some sort of rifle. He felt its heft in his hands, hoisted
it onto his shoulder, peered through the sight and

aimed the gun at the fishing rods hanging overhead. I suppose I should have run in the opposite direction, but something held me there.

It didn't take long for him to notice me. "Hey. It's the tree hugger," he said with a smirk.

I smirked right back at him. "Going hunting?"

"You bet," he said. "Bear hunting."

"Smokey or Yogi?"

He squinted at me through those heavy lids of his. "Lemme guess. You're not just a tree hugger, you're a save-the-whales type too."

He ran his hand over his short hair and shook his head. "Actually, it's Alaskan brown bear. Heading out to the Canadian coastal range." He lifted the second gun to his shoulder and pointed it at the sleeping bags on the wall. "Nothing like an Alaskan brown bear. Biggest sonofabitch I ever laid eyes on. Stands eight feet tall on his hind legs. Twelve hundred pounds of pure terror." He put the gun down. "Wanna come along? I could use a good cook."

I can't believe he asked me that. What a sexist jerk! "I think I'll pass, if it's all the same to you," I told him. I started to leave.

"What about those trees?" he called out.

I ignored him. I can't stand hunters. I think I'll write him a nice long e-mail and tell him exactly what I think of people who kill innocent animals for sport.

'Til next time,

V

August 8

I'm determined to be nicer to Lynette Kohl-Chase. So I dragged out the pressure cooker and made a pot of my mother's chili (from scratch), baked some cornbread (from mix), and toted it over to Lynette's house, feeling rather pleased with myself.

Lynette greeted me with a grimace. "I was just about to call you," she said, leading me into her characteristically immaculate kitchen. A sterling tea set was neatly arranged on a folded blue kitchen towel. A tub of silver polish and flannel cloth sat beside them. "You're so ambitious," I told her.

Lynette peeled off her yellow rubber gloves while I set the chili on her sparkling white cooktop. "It's the second Tuesday of the month," she explained matter-of-factly, laying the gloves over the edge of the sink. "Polishing day."

"And what's the third Tuesday of the month?" I teased.

"Ceiling fans and baseboards," she replied without missing a beat. "But if I had your money, I'd hire someone to polish my silver and wash my baseboards and I'd be eating bon-bons in France. Or someplace far, far away from here."

My money. Who knows how much longer it would be mine? What if Roger wins custody of Pete? What if he convinces that fathers' rights fanatic into reversing our settlement so Pete can "live in the manner to which he has grown accustomed"? I didn't want to think about that now.

"So, you said you were just about to call me. Is everything okay?" I assumed Lynette would want to talk about her bizarre new sex life, but, actually, she wanted to talk about me.

"Roger's lawyer called me," she began, and I felt my lunch surge in my stomach. "He wants to take a statement from me," Lynette continued. "I think he's going to make me testify against you!"

"What do you mean?"

"Well, the lawyer—Sloan, I think his name was— asked me all kinds of questions. About you, what kind of mother you were, if you ever left Pete alone, if you had men at your house." Lynette rubbed her eyes. "He just kept asking and asking, one question after the other. He totally caught me off guard. I'm afraid I might have said the wrong thing. Oh, Valerie!" Lynette bit her lower lip and stared at me.

"What did you say, Lynette? Tell me what you said!" I felt myself teetering on the precipice of hysteria. I wanted to shake her by the shoulders.

"I don't remember exactly," Lynette said, her voice cracking. "I told him about Eddie, how I saw him maybe once or twice here. I mentioned the detective. . . ."

"What else, Lynette? What else did you tell him?"

She started crying and put her face in her hands. "Oh, Valerie, I'm afraid I've really messed things up for you."

Now I really was shaking her. "What did you say, Lynette?"

"I told him about the time the boys carved soap at your house. With real knives. He asked me if I felt comfortable letting my own son play at your house and I, I told him how after that whole knife thing, I hesitated letting Hunter play there because"—she choked and sobbed—"I didn't think you were attentive enough. And I was afraid the boys might get hurt."

"Oh, Lynette, you *didn't*." I gripped the edge of the counter to steady myself. I wanted to hate her, but she obviously hated herself enough for both of us.

"I'm so sorry, Valerie." She covered her face with her hands. "He said I had to tell the truth."

"Yeah, but did you have to dredge up ancient history? He didn't specifically ask about the knives, did he? You volunteered that one yourself, right? What were you thinking, Lynette? What the hell were you thinking?" I was shaking now. Dear God, I was going to lose Pete! I grabbed Lynette's cordless phone. "I've got to call my lawyer."

"Of course, of course, go ahead." Lynette stood back, stuffed a knuckle in her mouth and watched me dial. I told Omar everything.

"I can't say I'm surprised, given the way your luck has been going today," Omar said, sighing deeply.

"What do you mean?" I glanced at Lynette. She had resumed her silver polishing, listening in. She looked stricken.

"There's good news, and then I'm afraid there is very bad news," he said. His voice sounded weary.

"Go on," I told him.

"The good news is, we're not getting Willis," Omar said, and at first I felt my heart do a joyful cartwheel. This wasn't just good news, it was great news! I didn't think I had a chance with that fathers' rights zealot. "So what's the bad news?" I asked Omar.

"The bad news is that your ex-husband has had an ex parte hearing with Judge Brand."

"Speak English, Omar. What does that mean?" I had a feeling it was something really bad.

"It means that your husband had a private consultation with another judge. The one who's presiding over your case. *Ex parte* means that they met without you."

"Is that even legal?" I asked. How could it be?

"Yes. I'm afraid it's perfectly legal."

"Okay. But I'm still not sure why this is such bad news," I continued. "It's not as if this new judge is another fathers' rights fanatic, is he?"

"No. It's worse than that," Omar explained. "He's a bitter, vindictive man whose wife left him last year. For a woman."

"Maybe I'm dense, Omar, but I still don't see why that's a problem for me."

"Because Roger is claiming that you left him for the same reason. And he says he has proof." He paused. "Valerie, is there something you haven't told me?"

I had to laugh. A lesbian? Me? He might as well have

accused me of being an Olympic gymnast; in either case my body just isn't designed to work that way. "I don't think Roger's going to get much mileage out of this strategy," I told Omar. "He doesn't have a case."

"He has pictures," Omar said quietly.

"Pictures of what?"

"I don't know. All Sloan would say is that they've got photographic evidence. Apparently it was enough to persuade Brand to schedule a hearing to contest the current custody arrangement. He's going for full custody. And I'm afraid that the testimony from your friend there isn't going to help."

"Why don't we get our own character witnesses? Mary's aunt Esta?"

Omar sighed heavily. "We could fill a room with Roger Tisdale's sexual victims, but none of their testimony would go to his competence as a father." Omar paused. "Lynette didn't help you on that front either, by the way."

"What do you mean?"

"Why don't you ask her? Our hearing with Brand is set for next Wednesday at eleven. We can talk later. In the meantime, I want you to put on your thinking cap and see if you can't come up with some anecdotal evidence of Roger's incompetence as a father."

I eyed Lynette, who was intently swabbing an ornate sugar bowl with a Q-Tip. "What did your lawyer have to say?" she asked. She buffed the sugar bowl to a blinding sheen. The smell of my chili commingled with the Tarn-X was nauseating.

"He said that Roger is going for full custody. And he said that your testimony is quite likely to help him make his case. So thanks, Lynette. Thanks a lot." My head throbbed. I closed my eyes and rubbed my temples. "Lynette, is there anything else you want to tell me?"

"About what?"

"About your conversation with Roger's lawyer."

She began wiping down a silver serving tray.

"Lynette, would you quit polishing the goddamn silver and answer me?" I pushed the tray with my hand and knocked over the Tarn-X bottle, spilling its noxious contents onto the counter and floor.

Lynette grabbed a dish towel. "It's okay, it's okay," she said, soaking up the spill, though I had not apologized.

"What else did you say, Lynette? Please."

"Well, I told him about the whole soap carving thing, you already know that. And how Roger had a reputation for playing the field."

"What else?"

"Well, let's see . . ." Lynette scratched her head. "Not much else, I guess."

"Did Sloan ask you what you thought of Roger as a father? Whether he was a good father?"

She squinted as if trying to recall something deeply

buried in her memory banks, but we both knew that the answer was at the surface of consciousness. "Well, yes. He did."

"And . . . ?" I prodded.

"And I told him I thought that despite all his character defects, Roger was a wonderful parent, better than most men, better than lots of women. In fact—"

"Better than me?" I cut in.

Lynette cringed like a dog about to be smacked. "Yes. Better than you." She folded the flannel polishing cloth and placed it on the counter. "I meant, better in the sense that he was home with Pete while you were at work. He was a good dad, Valerie. You have to give him that."

I was suddenly overwhelmed with animus toward this woman who had a whole shelf in her family room devoted to kids' crafts, who made her own play dough, taught Hunter and Pete how to create glycerin soap embedded with plastic bugs, made stained-glass windows from old crayons and wax paper, built gingerbread houses from scratch while slouches like me made prefabs with graham crackers and let our boys run wild with kitchen knives. That sweet-faced, baseboard-scrubbing bitch! I wanted to strangle her.

Then I just lost it. I quickly grabbed the pot of chili and dumped it on her floor, and regretted it just as quickly. We both stared at the deep red mess, the meat and beans and chopped tomato spreading across her gleaming tile floor like blood. I grabbed a roll of paper

towels and fell to my knees. "I'm sorry, Lynette." I
started to cry. "I'm so sorry."

"God, no, don't apologize. You have every right to be
angry with me." She was crying too.

We were both on the floor now, wiping up my
mother's best chili. I felt so sad, so cursed. I'd married
a miserable bastard. I'd dated a lunatic. My father was
dead. My sisters were no comfort. I had no real friends
to speak of. My current boyfriend was nice enough, but
something ineffable was missing, something I couldn't
quite name but felt deeply. I felt so horribly alone.

"As long as I'm confessing, I might as well tell you
. . . Roger's lawyer asked whether you were involved
with any women."

I stopped wiping. "Okay . . . and what did you say?"

"Well, I have to admit, the question embarrassed
me. I was afraid that the next thing he'd be asking was
if I were involved with women, and I'd have to tell him
about Melanie and Wade and all that."

"So what did you say?"

"Nothing, really." Lynette looked down and kept
wiping. "Just that you were friends with that Diana.
And I knew she was a homosexual. But I doubted you
were involved with her. Sexually, I mean."

"Doubted? You couldn't say definitively? You don't
know that I like men?"

Lynette looked pained. "I know you like men, Valerie. But I don't know what goes on behind closed
doors."

"And is that what you told Sloan? That you don't know what goes on behind closed doors?"

"More or less."

'Til next time,
ᐯ

August 9

I've been free-associating on the subject of Roger As Lousy Dad. This is what I've come up with so far:

A good father recognizes his power as a role model. Therefore, ALL irresponsible behavior (cheating on wife, buying mail-order bride, screwing teenage girls) must be considered irresponsible parenting. Setting up second household (condo) takes time, energy, resources, attention away from child.

Roger let Pete eat junk food. He let him stay up late at night. Sometimes let him wander around house when he should have been in bed. Did these things because he was too busy writing, didn't have time to look after Pete. Just because Roger worked at home doesn't mean he was always attentive.

Irresponsible behavior re: violence? Taught Pete to box. Said it was okay to punch anyone who teased him. Max Hubbard called Pete a poophead. Roger told Pete to punch Max in the nose. Said, "One good punch will shut him up for good."

Left Pete home alone when he was napping. Justifiable? Pete had fever, Roger ran to neighbor's to get Children's Tylenol. Maybe not such a good example. I could have stayed home from work that day. Had crush on Eddie, didn't want to miss work. Better not mention this.

Roger let Pete watch stupid TV shows. *Xena,* wrestling, Nick at Nite. Didn't pay attention when Pete was flipping channels. Pete once landed on nude sex scene. Station was scrambled but Pete could see enough to point out, "Hey, those people are naked!"

I called Omar, read my list to him. He said I was scraping the bottom of the barrel. "What about Roger's depression?" Omar said.

"What about it?" I asked.

"Well, he's on medication for it, right?"

"He was, a while ago. After one of his plays flopped. He was in bed for two weeks. But that was before Pete was born."

"Oh. Too bad. Is he still on medication?"

"I don't think so."

"Has he been depressed since then?"

"I guess. On and off. At some point during the Alyssa thing he was pretty bad. But he refused to take anything for it."

"I think we can work with that," Omar mused. "Clinical depression. I think we can pull something together."

I felt a stony lump in my chest. "This doesn't feel right to me, Omar. As a therapist, I would never recommend against custody simply because someone was being treated for depression."

"Valerie, you'd better check your high-minded ethics at the door," Omar snapped, and it sucked the wind out of me. "Because you can bet your ex-husband and his lawyer will stop at nothing to get Pete—and get his money back too. Let's talk again early next week." Click.

'Til next time,

V

August 10

Michael called to tell me that his mother died. Although she'd been sick for some time, her death came suddenly and was not expected, at least not expected to happen last night. "At least she went in her sleep," I told him, hoping to comfort.

"But I didn't get the chance to say good-bye."

Mom and I stopped by the house with flowers and a coffee cake. His parents (or I should say, his father) lived in a tidy high ranch with blue shutters and a cluster of brightly colored birdhouses on the front lawn. As we stepped across the threshold I could have sworn I saw Diana scramble into the kitchen. I heard the back door slam.

"Who was that?" I asked Michael.

"Who was who?" he asked, taking the flowers and

cake from my arms. He looked tired but quite gorgeous in a periwinkle blue shirt and buttercream yellow tie.

"Who was the woman who just ran out the back door?" I said, peering around his shoulder.

Michael looked at me quietly. "I don't know. Probably one of the neighbors. They've been coming by all morning."

"Are you sure it wasn't Diana Pierce?"

He took a breath as if he was about to say something, then seemed to changed his mind and shrugged instead.

I went into the bathroom and called Diana on my cell phone. I got her machine. "It's me and my machine," she purred. "You know what to do."

I hung up.

When I walked back into the living room, I saw a man who looked like an older, slightly shorter version of Michael. He had a thick head of hair and sweet, smiling blue eyes. "Dad, this is Valerie Ryan. Val, this is my father, Bud."

I reached for a handshake but was pulled into a great bear hug. "So this is Valerie Ryan." He held me at arm's length and appraised me. "You told me she was pretty, but you lied. She's beautiful." He pulled me back into a hug. "Thank you for stopping by," he said. He was louder than Michael, more gregarious.

"You're welcome, Mr. Avila. It's the least we could do."

"Call me Bud, please. Better yet, how about Pop?"

I blushed. So did Michael. He looked at me and rolled his eyes. "Dad, please."

I introduced my mother. "Now I know where you get your good looks," Bud said, bending over to kiss my mother's hand. The gesture would have been disturbing—the man's wife just died, after all—but I recognized it as the product of a unique kind of elation that seems to accompany the death of someone who has been dying for a long, long time.

As my mother and Bud chatted in the kitchen, I sequestered Michael in the hallway. I was sure I'd seen Diana slip out of his house and I was determined to find out, once and for all, if he knew her. And how.

"Just be honest with me, Michael," I started. Apparently he was expecting this.

"Okay, Val. I know Diana. I've known Diana for a long time." He spoke the words plainly but his face was darkened by a profound sadness. I would never have guessed what he was about to tell me, but I knew it would change our relationship forever.

I quickly reviewed the possibilities. None was especially appealing. Michael knows Diana because . . .

1. They met at an Alcoholics Anonymous meeting.
2. He arrested her for driving while intoxicated/ shoplifting/cooking someone's books.
3. They were married in a former life.
4. They are siblings in this life.
5. They are lovers.

"Maybe we'd better find someplace quiet to talk," Michael said quietly. I followed him to the staircase, watched his muscular haunches move solidly up the steps and wondered whether I would ever know his body in any intimate way, ever see what he looks like without clothes, ever trace my fingers along his lean, hard lines or press my lips against his chest or kiss his eyelids, one and then the other.

He led me to a small bedroom at the end of the hallway, the kind of room one furnishes with old furniture too worn to show to company, too good to throw away. There was a small upholstered chair in mustard yellow, its seat flattened like a ruined soufflé. There was a small brown Formica desk and a dented beige metal filing cabinet. A dusty laminated bookcase held dusty artifacts of another era, a plastic rocket from the 1964 World's Fair, books like *The Naked Ape* by Desmond Morris, and a complete set of plastic Beatles statuettes with wobbly heads. The only other seating was the daybed, covered with a brownish comforter, which smelled like mothballs. I chose the ruined soufflé chair while Michael arranged himself uneasily on the edge of the daybed. He clasped his large hands in front of him and brought them to his lips, as if in prayer.

"Diana and I used to travel in the same circles, so to speak," he began. His face was already crimson and he was beginning to sweat. It was hard for me to watch him struggle through his words.

"What kind of circles?" I asked, though I was certain he'd say he knew Diana from AA.

He shifted uncomfortably and loosened his tie. "Homosexual circles, Valerie." He was watching my reaction. What was I supposed to say, that I'd always suspected no heterosexual man would know how to make a gorgeous combination of a buttercream yellow tie and periwinkle shirt?

"So, you're gay, then?" I asked. The room seemed smaller, hotter.

He sighed. "I've never had sex with a man. But I've never had sex with a woman, either, not since high school, though I think that was just to prove something to myself, to my friends, to the girl. My parents were religious. Our church was very clear about homosexuality. I decided that I couldn't be a homosexual. And I just took the entire subject and put it up on a high shelf and left it there. I decided that homosexuality was a choice, and it was a choice I refused to make. My deadbeat brother had already given my parents enough grief. I wanted to be a regular person. I wanted a family and a house and a cat. I just wanted a normal American life."

A house and a *cat?* A golden retriever, maybe. A black lab, an Irish setter, a German shepherd. I could even see a Jack Russell terrier. But a cat? I said nothing. I waited for him to continue.

"The thing is, gay men were attracted to me. They

seemed to know something I refused to acknowledge. A few years back another cop invited me to a party. I didn't realize it was a gay party. Or maybe I knew it but didn't want to admit it. So I could pretend I'd been duped into going, like I was there against my will. That's where I met Diana. She was Diana Pierce back then, before she switched to her mother's maiden name. Diana and I stayed in touch, mostly by e-mail. She knew I was struggling. She was supportive. Diana was one of the few people I could talk to."

"So where are you now with all this?" I asked, though the answer didn't matter at that point. Something inside me had drained away. As if a switch had been flipped, I felt my sexual interest in Michael stream out of my body through the soles of my feet. I suddenly saw him not as a future lover, but as a dear friend—a big, beautiful friend who would never share my bed. I wasn't angry, I didn't feel betrayed or confused; I felt none of the emotions one reads about in true-confession pieces about women who discover their husbands' true sexual identity after twenty-five years of marriage. Actually, I felt somewhat relieved—I finally understood why he hadn't made any moves, and it had nothing to do with my fat thighs. I could have looked like Catherine Zeta-Jones and it wouldn't have mattered. Michael Avila was gay. I felt him—the dream of a relationship with him—slip through my arms like mist.

"I'm determined to live a heterosexual lifestyle,"

Michael said, sounding as if he was trying to convince himself as much as convince me. "I'm trying to get some help through GARTH."

"Garth?" I wanted to appear interested but at this point I only wanted to go home and go to sleep. "Who's he?"

"It's not a he, it's an organization. Global Association of Reparative Therapists," Michael explained. "They help people like me."

"Uh-huh." Yes, I *had* heard of those people. They've got some rather credible psychiatrists and psychologists on their board. And they claim spectacular "change rates" of converting homosexuals "back" into heterosexuality. I paid no attention to their work. I never believed that sexual orientation was a choice. I thought that conversion therapy was pathetic, illusory, a waste of time.

I didn't tell that to Michael, though. He seemed so hopeful. It was sad, really. I left as politely as I could, assuring Michael we would stay in touch but skirting the issue of dating again. I respect his quest, even if I'm dubious, but would rather not be involved in this particular experiment.

I retrieved Mom and drove her home. She was enchanted by Bud. I decided not to tell her about Michael.

'Til next time,

V

August 14

Omar called. The hearing has been postponed. Judge Brand has pneumonia and is in the hospital. Omar is happy to have the extra time but I'm exasperated. I'm anxious to get this over with. In the meantime, I've decided to call Roger. Omar will kill me for approaching him on my own, but I have to find out about these pictures.

'Til next time,

V

August 15

I called Roger this morning. "Tell me about those pictures, Roger."

His response, believe it or not, was: "Talk to the hand 'cause the face ain't listening."

"Excuse me?"

"I said, talk to the hand, Valerie."

I took a deep breath, "Roger, I'm so happy to see that the new zygote in your life has instructed you in the lingo of her generation, but that expression only works when you're talking to someone in person. Furthermore, nobody even says that anymore. Nobody except forty-two-year-old geeks who are desperately hoping to recapture their youth by dating little girls."

Roger sighed heavily. "Are you quite finished now?"

"I want to know about those pictures, Roger. You know I'm not a lesbian!"

"Well, my darling ex-wife, say what you want about your sexual inclinations, but these pictures are hard to refute. There's you and my old friend Diana. One of you is naked. And you're both in bed. What's more to say?"

I thought back to the motel room fiasco. "I can't believe you had a private investigator follow me!"

"Don't flatter yourself, Valerie. I wouldn't waste that kind of money on a dolt like you. Actually, these pictures came to me quite by accident. Over-the-transom, as it were."

"What do you mean?"

"I mean, someone sent them to me. Unsolicited. You might say, in fact, that these pictures are like a gift from God."

I turned Roger's words over and over. The pictures, he said, were a gift from God. Roger has never been spiritual or religious and only invokes God in such exclamatory remarks as, "God, did you see that three-point shot?" Or, "God, you're not going to wear that awful dress, are you?" Or, "Oh God, I'm coming."

Then I realized: Diana must have been behind those pictures. Ever since she joined Alcoholics Anonymous it's been God this, God that. Diana had to have been behind this. I knew she couldn't be trusted. I wanted to kick myself for spending even more than a moment in that motel room with her. I tried to remember whether

I'd put myself in any incriminating poses. I remember that she was naked—who could forget that body?—and at one point she'd yanked me off balance and I'd tumbled next to her. Did she touch me? Did I touch her? I think she tried to give me a massage at one point, so they probably have pictures of that. Diana is the touchy-feely type, so it's likely she rubbed my leg or squeezed my arm, and maybe they've got pictures of that, too. My head hurt just thinking about it. I was going to lose custody of Pete. I knew it.

"Okay, Roger," I said. "I figured out your little mystery. You got the pictures from Diana, right? Fine. I should have known."

Roger let out a snicker. "Diana? Good guess, but a wrong guess. No, my sweet, Diana is clearly on your side now. And after looking at those pictures, I can certainly see why." He lowered his voice. "Ooooh. You little temptress, you."

"So it wasn't Diana, then?"

"I'm sorry, didn't you hear me the first time? Oh my, Valerie, I do believe it may be time for you to get yourself a hearing aid. Don't be vain, my sweet. If you need one, buy one. You clearly have the money. At least you do now." I heard Surfer Girl's hysterical giggling in the background. "Now, if you don't mind, I have some business of my own to attend to."

I heard the girl laughing again and then a muffled squeaking of bedsprings. "Not now, sweetheart," Roger said. "Not now!" I was definitely not in the mood for this. I was expecting my period any day. I was homicidal.

"Come on, Rog," I heard her say. "Hang up the phone." She must have wrested the receiver from him. "Mrs. Tisdale—oops, I mean, *Ms.* Ryan, I forgot you were a feminist, Roger told me all about how you wouldn't take his name and all. Hey, want to guess what I'm doing to your ex-husband? Here. Just listen." There was a slurping noise, humming, and a low groan. And then a click. I knew I should have hung up first.

How stupid of me to assume that my problems with Roger were over the day I divorced him. The divorce was only the beginning of the torment. If he wins custody of Pete . . . I can't let myself contemplate it. Roger may be impoverished, but he's in a relationship with someone who adores him and he's having hot sex while I'm dating a guy who couldn't have sex with me if I paid him.

It's been so long since I had sex I'm beginning to play weird little mind games. I stay up at night watching CNN and wonder whether Dick Cheney is a good lover. Or I indulge in the masochistic game I love to hate, my own perverse variation of the Dating Game. I'll be sitting in some waiting room across from three motley-looking men and ask myself this question: If I absolutely had to sleep with one to save myself from the electric chair, who would I choose? The redneck with the stringy hair and dirty bandana and missing teeth? The chubby guy with the comb-over? Or the monkey man with the hairy neck and knuckles?

I know there are other ways of releasing all this steam, but the last time I used my electric boyfriend I think it gave me carpal tunnel syndrome and I just don't have the physical energy to go unplugged. I need something fast, clean, mindless.

'Til next time,

V

August 16

I've been a very naughty girl.

I'd finally gotten an estimate from a tree-relocation company. These people come and dig up your old tree and replant it somewhere else. It would cost me twelve thousand dollars to move the sycamores three feet onto my property. At this point, I didn't care how much it would cost. I wanted to save those trees, and I wanted Bill Stropp to shut the hell up already. I sent him an e-mail:

```
The trees will be moved, at a cost of
$12,000, incidentally. I hope this
resolves the issue, once and for all.
Valerie Ryan
```

I got this message back:

I want your assurance that you will also
take care of the holes those trees leave
behind. I want them filled and reseeded,
on the same day of removal. I don't want
you leaving behind any gaping holes on
my property. Understood?
Bill Stropp

Aarrrggghhh! He was impossible! I e-mailed him:

The area will be filled and seeded at my
expense. I would never leave any holes
behind. Understood? [I couldn't resist
adding that].
Valerie Ryan

Within moments, I received this e-mail from him:

Just make sure you fill the holes with
topsoil, and seed with turfgrass. None
of this rye crap.
Bill Stropp

That did it! I'd had enough of Bill Stropp. I hopped
in my Jeep and drove around the block to Cheshire
Lane. I strode up the path to his door. I had no idea
what I would say, I only wanted to scream at him, to

beat my fists against his chest, to tell him he had a lot of nerve, ordering me around like a servant. I rapped on the door and waited. He swung open the door and smiled as if he'd been expecting me.

"What is your goddamn problem?" I yelled.

"I don't have a problem," he said calmly, still smiling.

"Oh no?" I yelled. He must have been working out; there was a sheen of sweat sparkled across his shoulders and arms. He was wearing a black ribbed tank top and gray sweatpants, socks and Nike slides. He stepped toward me so we were inches apart, and I noticed he smelled clean and sweet.

"Uh-uh," he said, slowly shaking his head. His eyes slowly appraised me. "It's hot out. You maybe want to discuss this inside?"

So I stepped inside. And when he closed the door behind me, I don't know what got into me, but I grabbed Bill Stropp's face and kissed him full on the mouth, and he kissed me back, and before I knew it, we were against the wall, and my hand was down his sweatpants and he felt hot and hard and wonderful. We had sex against that wall, and again on the floor, and once more somewhere else, I can't remember where, and I haven't stopped thinking about him since I left his house six and a half hours ago and I can't believe how good I feel.

'Til next time,

V

August 17

It was about noon when the doorbell rang. I assumed it was Lynette; she said she wanted to drop off a loaf of Friendship bread and starter. (I have a theory about Friendship bread, by the way. Since it's more like cake than bread, you wind up eating the whole loaf in one sitting. What kind of friend would give you a loaf of bread, knowing full well that you'll eat it all yourself in one sitting? The kind of friend who doesn't want to see you release the thin person within, I say.)

I yanked the door open, ready to accept my Friendship Loaf. It wasn't Lynette, it was Diana, wearing a red leather cowboy hat, red leather miniskirt, and a fringed red leather halter top. The only misstep in her ensemble was a canvas tote bag, the kind you get for making a fifty-dollar donation to public radio. "Well, howdy!"

"You've got a lot of nerve, showing up here like this," I blurted out.

Diana's eyes widened. "What? What did I do?"

"You know exactly what you did, Diana. Don't you dare try to bullshit me."

"Hey," she said, raising her hands as if in surrender. "You've got the wrong guy. Whatever I did to you in the past, I've made my amends. I'm a good girl now. You know that."

"Really? Then how did Roger get his hands on pictures of us in the Econolodge? Pictures he intends to use to win full custody of my son!"

Diana reeled back. "Valerie. Honest to God, I have no idea. Are you sure he has pictures? How do you know? Oh my God. I can't believe this. I'm the one who's *naked* in those pictures."

"No kidding, Diana. And I was sitting next to you. On the bed. But what do you have at stake, really? You don't have kids. You don't have a husband. You've already wrecked your career." Diana looked injured, and I knew then that she had nothing to do with the pictures. "Roger said they came in over the transom. Like a gift from God, he said."

"We're going to get to the bottom of this," she said, marching into the house. "Let me call Omar. I'll find out who's behind this."

"Omar doesn't know," I told her. "And Roger's not telling."

"But I bet Roger's lawyer knows," Diana said excitedly, tossing her hat and coat onto the sofa and laying her tote bag gingerly on the dining room table. "And I bet I can get him to tell me."

"You know Richard Sloan?"

"I sure do." Diana had pulled the phone book out of the kitchen drawer and was running her finger down a column of numbers. "I know Sloan very well. And, baby, he owes me. Big time. The least he can do is tell me where he got the pictures." She punched in the number and looked at me, grinning.

"That can't be ethical, can it?" I wondered what was in the bag. It didn't smell like food. Not that I had an appetite.

"Ethical, shmethical." Diana snorted. "He'll tell me." She stopped.

"Mr. Sloan, please." Diana tapped her fingers restlessly on the kitchen counter. I tried to sneak a peek at her bag but she pulled it away before I could reach it.

"Richie? How are you, sweetheart?" she began, grinning at me. "Fine, wonderful. Loving life, living right, one day at a time." She twisted her hair girlishly. "Listen, Richie, I've got a favor to ask. You know those pictures? Yes, those are the ones. Uh-uh. Thanks. Yeah, I've been working out. Look, darling, I'm not asking you to burn those pictures—though I'd be forever in your debt if you would. I'd just like to know where you got them. . . . Don't make me beg, baby. . . . Uh-uh. . . . I see. . . . You're a gem. Thanks, Richie. Love to Jazzie." She hung up the phone and stared at me. "Oh. Val. You're going to love this."

"What, Diana? Just tell me. Where did Roger get those pictures?" My heart stopped. "Who sent them?"

"Your old spiritual advisor," Diana said. "Reverend Lee."

"Very funny," I said, certain she was joking. "No, really. Who sent Roger the pictures?"

Diana plucked a red grape off the bunch on the counter and popped it in her mouth. "I told you. His Holiness. The good pastor. Reverend Lee."

"You're kidding."

"Why would I make that up?" She popped another grape into her mouth. "So tell me. What's a nice little pastor doing in an Econolodge, snapping pictures of you and me in bed?"

"We weren't in bed, Diana."

"You know what I mean," she said, rolling her eyes. "Why would he follow you to the motel? Did he have the hots for you? Come on, Val, put on your little thinking cap and figure it out."

So I thought about it. And I had to conclude that no, absolutely not, Reverend Lee had never been attracted to me. See, I pride myself on my finely tuned pheromone detector. I can usually tell when I've perked a chemical reaction, and Reverend Lee never tripped my radar, much as I might have wanted him to. I was grateful for any man's attention, and when Reverend Lee took my hand in his to pray, the warmth was as seductive as a stare. But back then I was happy to have my dentist's fat fingers in my mouth. As I said, I was grateful for any man's attention.

"Not possible," I said finally.

"Richie Sloan wouldn't lie to me." She handed me the phone. "Call the good Rev and find out what's going on."

I stared at the phone. I was paralyzed.

"Fine," Diana said impatiently. "Then I'll call." She grabbed the phone book. "Which church?"

"First United Methodist. On East Lattimer."

I watched Diana punch in the numbers. "It's ringing," she said. Then she handed me the phone. "You talk to him."

I picked it up just as Lila the secretary answered. "First United," she sang. "How can I help you?"

"Uh, er, is Reverend Lee there?" I stammered.

"May I tell him who's calling?" the secretary chirped.

"It's Valerie. Valerie Ryan."

"Sure, Miss Ryan. Hold on just a moment."

I watched Diana pop another grape into her wide mouth and I waited. How would I start? What would I say? What if Sloan was lying? I had to proceed with caution, couldn't just accuse him outright, couldn't assume anything.

"Valerie!" Reverend Lee's voice was bright, unsuspecting. "Long time, no see! How are you?"

How was I? Happy to be divorced from Roger, petrified that I might lose my son, exhilarated by a new affair, miserable that Roger and his girlfriend remain fixtures in my life, sickened by the possibility that this new judge might reverse our divorce settlement. "I'm fine," I told him.

"Wonderful!" he responded. "That's wonderful."

"No. That's a lie. I'm not fine. I'm quite upset, to be honest. Upset and confused."

"Do you want to talk about it?" he said, in that soothing pastorial voice of his.

"Yes."

"Shall we set up an appointment, then?" The man didn't have a clue.

"Actually, I was hoping we could talk now." I felt my adrenaline surge.

"I've got a few minutes. Shoot."

I inhaled deeply. Diana squeezed my arm and mouthed, "You can do this."

"Reverend Lee, you know that Roger and I are divorced, and I have primary custodial rights. Well, Roger is now contesting those rights. He wants full custody. And he's doing everything in his power to get it. He's claiming I'm gay. And he apparently has pictures of me in a hotel room, with someone who happens to be lesbian, and I'm afraid those pictures have put me in a compromising position, if you know what I mean." I waited for a reaction.

"Oh, Valerie, I'm sorry." That was empathy, not an apology. He really had no idea what I was about to say.

"I tried to find out where the pictures came from."

"Yes . . . ?"

"And apparently they came from you?"

Silence. Then, finally, "Say that again?"

"I said, Reverend Lee, the pictures came from you. *You* sent those pictures to my ex-husband."

"Valerie, I realize that you've been under enormous stress, what with the divorce and all. And sometimes when we're under that kind of stress, we say things we can't possibly mean. Things that don't make sense."

I didn't think he was lying. I honestly believed he was as confounded as he appeared to be, as I was. I began to wonder if Richard Sloan had lied to Diana. I looked at her. Her eyes lit up. She frantically pulled a pad and pen out of my junk drawer and scribbled, *Is Rev married?*

I nodded.

Happily? Diana wrote. I shrugged. How the hell should I know? Then I remembered that I'd heard they were once separated. I thought back to the times Michelle had answered the phone, how irritated and put-upon she always sounded. Michelle was hardly the model pastor's wife. She often skipped services, and rarely participated in church functions. Diana was scribbling again: *Maybe wife sent pics?*

"Reverend Lee, I believe you when you say you had nothing to do with those pictures, I really do. But I've got to ask this: Do you think your wife might have had anything to do with this?"

He didn't say anything for a long time. "Reverend?" I prodded.

"Maybe," he said heavily. I flashed Diana a thumbs-up.

"Do you mind if I talk with her?" I said.

"We're separated. Again. I'm not sure I even know where she is."

"Reverend Lee, can you tell me why your wife would have followed me to a motel room? Please?"

The reverend brought his mouth closer to the phone

and whispered, "I can't talk about this now. Not here. Can we meet somewhere?"

He told me he had to prepare for a board meeting tonight and wouldn't be available until tomorrow. I arranged to meet him at Pony's, 11 A.M.

When I got off the phone I was desperate to do something, anything, to feel like I was in control of my life. I wanted to go online, search for Michelle Lee. Maybe I could find an e-mail address, a phone number, a police record, who knows?

"Forget it," Diana said. "Don't waste your time. You'll wind up with seventeen thousand sites about *Knot's Landing*." She reached for her tote bag. "Here. I brought something for us to do."

I froze.

She saw the look on my face. "Don't worry, silly billy. It's nothing like that. Here. Come check this out."

I watched as Diana pulled out the following objects from her bag: a large white pillar candle, a bunch of dried herbs tied with raffia, a box of red-tipped matches, and a heavy crucifix. "What's all this?" I asked.

Diana smiled at me. "It's everything you need for a home exorcism. Everything but the priest. But I've been assured that this do-it-yourself kit works just as well."

"What are you talking about?"

"I'm talking about evil, baby. Malevolent forces. Dark spirits." She struck a match against the sole of her boot and lit the white candle. "I'm talking about Roger."

"You have to be kidding. Now you're into wicca?"

Diana turned off the fluorescent kitchen light. "Not really. But I really do believe that old lovers and husbands leave behind bad mojo. You know, like an odor." She opened a window in the dining room, letting in the balmy air. "So I went online, looked up purification rituals. This is sort of a mishmash of different rituals, but I think it should work."

"Jeez."

"Lighten up. It'll be fun." Diana tipped the edge of the herb bundle into the flame, let it burn a moment, then blew it out. It smoked like incense. "This is sage. Got it at the health food store. Now close your eyes."

"No."

"Come on, Val. Work with me here."

I closed one eye and peeked with the other. Diana waved the sage over her head and began a slow spiral in the middle of the room. She chanted:

"Come ye spirits, come white raven,

Cleanse this home, this hearth, this haven—"

She looked at me. "Isn't this great? I made it up myself."

She continued,

"Evil spirits, now depart.

I call upon the clear white heart.

Darkness, blackness, gloom and doom

Take heed for now I cleanse this room.

The sun doth shine upon our star,

Yada, yada, yada . . . something, something, from afar.

In the name of the Goddess, I cast this spell
And send Roger Tisdale to the flames of hell!"

Diana ended her dance with a dramatic twirl. She leaned toward the candle and blew it out with a loud whoosh. She inhaled deeply and exhaled noisily. "I can feel it, can't you?"

"Feel what?"

"The absence of Roger's malevolent spirit. The air feels cleaner somehow, doesn't it?"

I made a face and shrugged. The truth is, I think she's right.

'Til next time,

V

August 18

2:10 A.M. I can't sleep. So I put on CNN. But I didn't want to wake Pete, so I switched on the closed captioning. I feel sorry for anyone who relies on closed captioning. Here's a sample of the mumbo jumbo that scrolled across my TV set:

As Americans fear a recession, Plesdentn Tush has pront to speed yup his tax clot to help get the faltzeloing econom back o tyrack.

A convicted terrorist and former ally of Saudi xsmile Osamee benslattin will beeee the government's first witness in trail ooops trial of the bombings of mbassy.

Tomorrow I meet Reverend Lee. And find out why his wife is involved in this mess.

'Til next time,

V

August 18, later

I've decided that the best way to start the day is with aerobic activity. Tae-Bo works well. Sex works better. Bill called at 8:35, a moment after Pete's bus pulled away. By 8:39 I was riding his strong, sweaty body like a bronco. By 10:30 I was showered, moisturized, blow-dried, made up, fully dressed, and on my way to meet Reverend Lee.

As I drove downtown, as I popped a couple of quarters in the meter, as I strode up the block, a joyous voice in my head sang, "I'm having sex! Hallelujah! I'm having sex! Amen!" (to the tune of "It's Raining Men"). I don't want to know about Bill Stropp's ex-wife and kids, I don't want to know about his tire stores or his favorite foods or childhood traumas. We are two bodies, joined in a mutual quest for pleasure, release, satisfaction. Period.

When I arrived for my meeting with Reverend Lee, the restaurant was still empty. Busboys were setting up the tables for lunch as the manager adjusted the blinds, letting in bright shafts of sunlight. Reverend Lee was sitting in a booth in the far back, in the smoking section. I knew he didn't smoke, so I assumed he chose that table for the privacy. He stood and waved. He smiled nervously. "Coffee?"

"Sure," I told him. Reverend Lee signaled the waiter, a lanky college kid with a high forehead and dark blond ponytail. We both watched as he filled my cup, then topped off Reverend Lee's.

"I'm definitely ready for colder weather," he said. I must have heard that line fifty times in the last month. It's all anyone says around here. It's the standard conversation starter, a classic example of small-town talk. I always nod, agree, say something vacuous like, "No kidding." But, in truth, I couldn't wait for winter. I think I could handle twelve months of winter, twelve months of oversized sweaters and leggings with elastic waistbands, coats and jackets that camouflage my wide-load ass.

Enough weather talk. "Reverend Lee, what's going on here?"

He stared into his coffee cup as if the answers might materialize in the clouds of half-and-half. "I can only speculate," he began. He took a long breath, kept staring into his cup. "Michelle is a very jealous woman." He took a sip and set the cup down again. "Nine years ago, when I was assistant pastor at Faith Methodist in Owensboro, there was . . . an indiscretion . . . with a congregant." He looked at me. "So you see, Michelle comes by it honestly. Her jealousy, I mean."

I thought about the times I'd called him at home, and how resentful Michelle had sounded when I asked to speak with her husband. "So you think she's behind the pictures?"

"She is. She had you followed."

"She hired a private investigator?"

He nodded. "She has pictures of us in my office, holding hands, praying together. And she has pictures of me in your house after Mary died."

I shivered.

"But the only really, uh, scandalous pictures were the ones taken at the Econolodge, and those are the ones she sent Roger."

"But you weren't in those pictures!"

Reverend Lee shrugged. "Michelle didn't care. She'd convinced herself that we were involved. She hated you. She wanted to hurt you." Reverend Lee reached for my hand. "I don't know what to say, Valerie. I'm so terribly sorry."

You damn well should be, I wanted to scream. You screw around and I wind up paying for it!

At this point I ask myself: Was I born under a freaking dark star? Have I been cursed by the gods? Am I trapped in some kind of ancient karmic purgatory of sin and retribution? Why me, oh Lord, why me? Why are all these people always apologizing to me for some form of deception and betrayal? Why can't I live a normal, uneventful Midwest suburban life? Why can't I simply wake up every morning next to my stable, balding husband, send Pete off to school, eat my bowl of Special K, vacuum my house, make a casserole for the church potluck, whip up a nutritionally complete dinner, have missionary sex with my stable, balding husband, and go to sleep? Not me. I wound up with the Philandering Shithead Formerly Known As My Husband. And everything else just flows like sludge from that singular mistake.

"Now what the hell am I going to do?" I said. I was too overwhelmed to cry. I wanted to go home and go to sleep.

"I don't suppose you want to join me in prayer?"

I stared at Reverend Lee's kind, bland face and repressed the urge to rip it off. "Maybe some other time."

'Til next time,

V

August 19

I called Libby as soon as Pete left for camp. I had to know how it was logistically possible to get those pictures.

"Hmmmm," she said, considering my question. "Even with the blinds or curtains closed, I can usually get a clear shot depending on the angle and if I've got the right lense," she said. "All you really need is a little crack between the blinds."

Shit.

Interestingly, it seems that my libido intensifies in direct proportion to the level of stress in my life. Bill called at noon and summoned me. We had sex in silence, hungrily, against the foyer wall. We kept our clothes on. As I left, he said, "Forget about the trees," and I said, "Okay." Those were the only words we exchanged.

'Til next time,

V

August 20

Pete is home with a stomach virus. I cleaned vomit off the carpet and all the bedding, replaced the sheets and pillowcases, and got him back into bed. Then he threw up again. I've got him in the guest room now. I put on Nickelodeon, but he's too miserable to enjoy it. Poor little guy. I think I hear him calling me. Gotta go.

I'm back. I was on my hands and knees scrubbing puke out of the kilim rug in the guest room when the phone range. It was Omar. My custody hearing is Monday.

'Til next time,

V

August 21

Omar and I met to talk strategy. He believes it's likely that:

- Sloan will argue that it's in Pete's best interests to live full time with Roger because of my "immoral" lesbian lifestyle.
- Sloan will produce Exhibit A, the photographs of me and Diana at the motel room.
- Omar says it's unlikely that he will have pictures of Eddie and me in that same motel room, because it doesn't bolster the lesbian angle.
- In addition to arguing for full custody, Sloan will request an immediate full reversal of the settlement, and I will be asked to repay whatever money I have already spent. (I almost had a heart attack when I heard this, but Omar insists that even under the worst circumstances, the judge won't make me pay back the money).
- Sloan will support his case with testimony and comments from various witnesses such as Lynette.

Omar has assured me that Roger will NOT get everything he wants. But by asking for full custody, he is likely to get at least joint custody. By arguing for a settlement reversal, he's likely to get at least alimony or child support. Omar says that because we already have a sympathetic judge (sympathetic to Roger, that is) we must tread lightly on character issues. In other words, we'll need to be careful in raising Roger's infidelity/bigamy as an issue. As Omar put it, "If it doesn't go to his competence as a father, it's worthless." Omar's key strategy:

- The photographs do not prove a lesbian relationship. Omar will present Diana's sworn statement verifying that she and I have never had a sexual relationship.
- Pete needs the stability of one home, with his mother, the parent who has cared for him during this entire ordeal.
- My current financial situation enables me to stay home with Pete and give him my undivided attention.
- Roger's sexual activity and former "marital relationship" with a minor has made it difficult, if not impossible, for Roger to be an attentive and responsive father.

I'm trying not to obsess about this, but I'm consumed by questions. If Roger gets full custody, am I going to be closed out of Pete's life? Will Roger's zygote du jour become his new mommy? (I swear, I could kill myself just thinking about that.) If Roger wins joint custody, how will Pete handle the stress of shuttling back and forth between two households? What if Pete gets angry with me and decides he doesn't want to come back here? How will I oversee Pete's emotional/moral/ethical development if I'm not the main caregiver in his life? What if Roger and his zygote let him run wild, let him watch limitless TV, eat only junk food . . . or worse—smoke pot. Drink beer. Join the skateboarding street kids in the municipal parking lot.

I'm driving myself crazy. I've got to get some sleep.

'Til next time,
ꝗ

August 22

Oh God. Pete walked in while I was pulling my custody files together. He picked one up, spotted his name, and tried to read through the legalese. He couldn't. He asked me to read it to him. I told him as simply as possible that I was going to court to make sure that he would stay with me, but he would still get to visit with his father. He started to cry. He said he didn't want to visit Roger. He wanted to live with him! I asked him, "You mean, you want to live with both of us?"

"No, I mean, I want to live with Daddy. But you can come visit us whenever you want."

I decided not to pursue it. Pete can say whatever he wants. I'm not giving him up.

'Til next time,
ꝗ

August 24

It's 2:15 A.M. and I cannot fall asleep. I suppose I could have taken something but then I'd be logy tomorrow and I can't afford that. So I'm sitting here, imagining what life would be like without Pete, torturing myself, really, picturing his empty room, empty bed. We had a perfect evening together. I made his favorite meal (pot roast, glazed carrots, mashed potatoes, Ben & Jerry's chocolate fudge brownie ice cream for dessert), got a fire going (okay, I cheated. I used a Duraflame log) and then we played four rounds of Cootie. As I tucked him in, I asked, "Did you mean it when you said you wanted to go live with Dad?"

He blinked sleepily. "I dunno."

"Well, it's okay if you feel that way, sweetie," I told him. "Your feelings are never wrong. You can feel anything you want and it's okay. But I hope you understand that we need to make choices that will be best for you." I was on unsteady ground now. I didn't want to bad-mouth Roger. That's a lie. I wanted to say, Your dad is a bad man, Pete. He is a pathological philanderer with a predilection for young flesh. He trampled on his marriage vows. He had an illegitimate wife and now has a girlfriend young enough to be your big sister. And if you wind up living with him I will absolutely kill myself.

"But I love my dad." His bottom lip trembled. "I miss Dad. How come I never get to see him anymore?"

If there is any justice in this world, there will be a special circle in hell reserved just for Roger and his ilk. Bad enough that he betrayed me. I'll survive. I can't say the same for Pete. "Dad never stopped loving you, sweetie. And he is fighting hard to see more of you. But . . ." I swallowed hard. "Daddy has problems, honey, and those problems make it hard for him to be the kind of daddy you deserve to have."

Pete sat up. "I don't care if Dad has problems. I wanna be with him. And he wants to be with me. And if you try to stop him, I'm gonna hate you forever!"

My son's words stung like a slap. I willed myself to stay calm but I could feel tears flood my eyes. "Well, sweetie," I began, "you're very angry. I can see that. But I still love you. I will always love you. And Daddy will always love you too. And somehow we're going to work this out and maybe it won't be so easy or fun all the time, but you will always be loved and cared for because you are very precious to us. Do you understand that?"

Pete turned his head to the wall and said nothing.

"Pete?"

"Can you bring me a glass of water, please? And a Milano cookie?"

I guess the conversation was over for now. I went down to the kitchen. I wondered whether I was, indeed, doing the right thing by Pete in fighting for full custody. I called my mother to get her advice and she told me I'd be crazy—not just crazy, but irresponsible—if I didn't push for full custody.

Now it's 2:25 A.M. and I have to be in court in seven and a half hours and I'm too tired and worried and scared to sleep. I've got to try.

It's 3:20 A.M. I am still awake. Even C-SPAN didn't

put me to sleep. I'm going to make myself a cup of chamomile tea.

'Til next time,

V

August 25

The tea worked. I fell asleep on the family room sofa and even though I didn't have an alarm clock, I miraculously woke in time to get Pete dressed, fed, and on the bus. He didn't say anything else about the custody issue, and I didn't bring it up. I wanted him to go to school unencumbered by worry, though I suspect he's plenty encumbered already.

I called Omar for wardrobe advice. How does a good mother dress these days? "For starters, don't wear slacks or sensible shoes," he said. "We don't want to re-inforce any lesbian stereotypes. No plunging necklines, nothing too form-fitting. And don't wear a suit. We don't want you looking like a corporate executive. A little makeup, but not too much."

Maybe I should wear an apron. I could wheel in one of those portable cooktops, the kind they use for demonstrations at gourmet shops. I could prepare chicken piccata during the hearing—thus proving that I'm not merely a fine cook, but a model multitasker. "So what *should* I wear?" I said, sighing heavily.

"Hard to say for sure. The judge is a tough nut. You

don't want to look like you're trying too hard. That's the sort of thing he'd pick up on. Hmmmm."

I waited. I felt like scratching my flesh off.

"Okay. Denim skirt, or corduroy jumper, something soft, something with flowers. No cleavage, obviously. No minis. Or skip the patterns altogether. Solid pastels. No checks. Nothing black. Does that help?"

"In other words, I should dress like the Easter Bunny."

Omar chuckled. "I'm glad you haven't lost your sense of humor. That's a good sign."

"I don't have anything that fits your description." I didn't mention the denim skirt I bought at Paul Harris, the one that made me feel like I was wearing sausage casing. My hips weren't just wide in that skirt, they were elephantine. And it was designed for minimum mobility—I could only take baby steps, not great big confident Charlie perfume strides. I tried to think back to my breast-feeding support group—aka the Cult of Motherhood. What did those women wear? The only thing I remember about that group was that (1) one of the women used to say "umbiblical cord" and no one corrected her; (2) they persevered with me until Pete finally latched onto my painfully engorged breasts; (3) they encouraged us to breast-feed indefinitely, even if your child is old enough to pull up a chair and do the *New York Times* crossword puzzle between breasts; (4) nobody except me wore makeup.

"You're a resourceful woman. I'm sure you'll think of

something," Omar said. "I'll meet you outside courtroom number four." He paused. "Ms. Ryan?"

"Yes, Mr. Sweet?"

"We're going to be fine."

"If you say so, Omar." It is now 8:45 and I still have
no idea what I'm going to wear.

August 25, evening

Jesus, what a day.

When I got to the courthouse (wearing one of
Lynette's yellow corduroy jumpers—she wore it when
she was pregnant with Hunter), Omar looked worried.
"What's wrong, Omar?"

"Nothing. It's fine. We're going to be fine."

"Really. Tell me."

"Well," he began, running a finger under his
starched collar, "it's Judge Brand. He's in a foul mood
this morning."

We heard the *click-click* of Judge Brand's tiny wingtips
as he hurried up the corridor toward courtroom number
four. He looked like a ferret. Beady black darting eyes,
slicked-down dull brown hair, a Hitlerian mustache
wedged between his nose and upper lip. He scowled
and appraised me with cold, miserly eyes. He nodded
toward Omar. "Let's get started, shall we?"

Omar went to get a drink at the water fountain.
"Good morning, Mizz Ryan." It was Surfer Girl. Her hair
was even longer than I'd remembered it. She'd pulled it

into two long braids on either side of her head. She wore a short white Pleather skirt and matching jacket, a glittery white camisole, white tights, and shiny black platform boots. She made a scratchy gagging sound. She reached into her mouth with her long fingers and pulled out something and held it to the light. It was a pale curly pubic hair. I recognized it right away. In fact, I'm still cleaning those freaking hairs out of the bathroom drain. Surfer Girl shrugged. "Occupational hazard, I guess." She moved toward the courtroom. She paused at the door. "By the way," she said, "you have an adorable little boy. I can't wait to get to know him."

"Fuck you." I wanted to kill her. Omar reappeared and pushed open the heavy door and gestured for me to enter before him. The room was freezing and I later learned that Brand insists on setting the thermostat to sixty-two degrees.

"Where is everybody?" I asked Omar. My mother was supposed to be there, as were Diana and Lynette.

"It's still early. Be patient."

Sloan was there, with two assistants, a thirtyish woman wearing a drop-dead gorgeous aubergine silk suit and a young, equally attractive man who wore a crisp white shirt and maroon suspenders. I felt like such a jackass in my yellow corduroy jumper. "Don't you have any assistants?" I whispered to Omar. He smiled benevolently and put a reassuring hand over mine. "We're fine, Val," he whispered. Roger swiveled his head around and winked at me. Bastard!

Suddenly the doors swung open. A man and woman stepped tentatively inside. "Is this courtroom four?" the man asked in a thick Southern accent. He was short and fidgety, with a bushy black beard and heavy-rimmed glasses. The woman with him had a white-blond Ivana do, her hair was swept up and held in place with a heavy gold clip.

Omar stepped forward. "You must be Kelia's parents." He extended a hand. "I'm so glad you could make it."

I heard Roger whisper to his lawyer, "What the hell are *they* doing here?"

Omar flashed me a jubilant smile. Surfer Girl's parents were there to testify. Based on Roger's horrified reaction, they were definitely *not* testifying on his behalf. "If you think this is good, just wait," Omar whispered. He squeezed my hand. "You'll never believe who's coming."

First witnesses: Surfer Girl's parents. They sat together at a small table on a low platform, an area designated as a kind of witness stand. Judge Brand began. "For the record, please state your names."

"George and Pookie Smith." The small man with the bushy beard spoke for both of them.

"Er, Pookie?" Brand asked.

"Yes. Pookie." The woman pulled herself up and stuck out her chin. "That's the name my mama gave me."

"Your relationship to Roger Tisdale?" Judge Brand continued.

George Smith hopped up in his chair. "I don't have a relationship and I don't want a relationship!"

"Oh, come on, Pop," Roger whined.

"Dammit, I told you not to call me Pop. You're as old as I am, for Christ's sake."

George Smith turned back to the judge. "Look, Your Highness—"

"Your Honor will do," Brand cut in.

"Sorry. Your Honor. Kelia always does what she wants; always did, always will. That's just the kind of kid she is. So one day she marches in with this guy and says he's moving in, so what am I going to say? If I tell her no, she moves away with him and shacks up somewhere else. But telling her yes, God a'mighty, it was the worst decision I ever made!"

Pookie shook her head sadly. "If it wasn't for Kelia, Roger Tisdale would be out on his butt in a heartbeat."

"Damn straight," George continued. His face was deep crimson. He pulled a handkerchief from his jacket pocket and swabbed his forehead. "He has no shame! One day I see them in the car in the driveway, going at it like a pair of rabbits, right in the driveway, right in front of our neighbors! Like it was nothing! Like it was nothing at all!"

Pookie pulled her handbag to her chest. "That man is ruining my daughter's reputation! And he leaves his socks everywhere, his filthy socks! I have enough work picking up after George. This is ridiculous!" Pookie shot Roger a disgusted look.

Omar took a sip of water and approached the table. "Mr. and Mrs. Smith, do you think Roger Tisdale is prepared to take on the responsibility of full-time fatherhood? Is Roger Tisdale fit to be a father?"

"Comes in all hours of the night," George Smith went on, muttering as much to himself as to anyone in the courtroom. "It's crazy, I tell ya. Here we are, three forty-year-olds and my daughter there, crammed into our itty-bitty house, acting like it's the most natural thing in the world. It's a freak show! This bum sits around, eating our food, drinking our beer, having his way with our little girl. Says he's writing his next big hit, but I don't see him doing diddly-squat! I told him, go get yourself a job! You're an able-bodied man. Hell, I could even get him a job at the shop if he wanted one. He could start working today if he'd get off that lazy ass of his."

Pookie leaned forward. "Kelia says he gets a nice check every month from his parents. One of those trust fund deals. Then we come to find out he doesn't get his check anymore because he's divorced."

"Seems his parents had the good sense to cut him off," George continued. "Then I hear him tell Kelia he's—how did he put it—oh, he says, 'Honey, I quite like slumming with your family.' *Slumming!* Can you believe that?" George pointed a stubby finger at Roger.

"I'll tell you something, buster, our house may be small but at least I have a house. And every month I pay the mortgage and I don't have bill collectors come knocking on my door."

Pookie put a hand on her husband's arm. "Take it easy, sugar."

"I'll repeat the question, sir," Omar continued. "Do you think Roger is fit to be a father?"

"Well, I sure as hell wouldn't want a father like him."

God, this was fun. Now it was Sloan's turn. He stepped forward and smiled patronizingly. "Mr. and Mrs. Smith. Thank you for coming today. How are you today?"

George smirked and rolled his eyes. "How the hell do you think I am?"

"It sounds like you've had your share of stress lately."

"Stress? Are you kidding? That's not the half of it." He reached over and patted his wife's hand. "It's been hell."

Sloan's smile froze. "I understand, sir. Clearly, you and Roger Tisdale aren't the best of friends."

"You're not getting the picture, buddy boy. I want that guy out of my house! Pronto!"

Sloan went on. "You've described a number of situations that you find annoying, and I can't blame you. But the purpose of our meeting today is to determine if Roger Tisdale has what it takes to make a good father. Mr. Tisdale's goal is to get full custody of his beloved son. Can you understand that? And let me urge you to answer the questions and refrain from elaborating. Just answer the questions, Mr. Smith. Are you aware that Mr. Tisdale's goal is to obtain full custody of his son?"

George Smith scowled and looked away. "Yes, I suppose so."

"So, the question, Mr. Smith, is this: Is there any reason to think Roger Tisdale is not fit to have custody of his son?"

"Well, how about his house? Doesn't a good father have a home for his child? I sure hope he doesn't expect to bring his kid into *our* house, because that's not going to happen, no sirree Bob. That's where we draw the line."

Pookie nodded enthusiastically. "I raised my babies already and I'm through with that," she chimed in.

"Well," Sloan went on, "let's assume that Roger and Pete won't be living with you. Let's assume that Roger will have enough money at that point to buy his own home where he and his son will live. Now, sir, do you have any reason to believe that Roger Tisdale would not make a fit parent?"

George Smith frowned and folded his arms across his chest. "I dunno, I guess I got no reason to think that."

Sloan stepped back and pivoted on his heel. "No further questions for the Smiths, Your Honor."

"I have a few more questions." Omar stood up.

"Thank you once again for coming. I know it's not easy taking off from work."

"Sure as hell isn't. I've got thirty-two vacuum cleaners that need fixin' and they're all due yesterday!"

"So obviously, for you to skip a day of work, this is pretty important, isn't it?"

"Sure as hell is."

"Mr. Smith, may I ask, what do you think of a forty-year-old man going after a girl half his age, sir?"

"I think it's shameful, is what I think!"

Sloan interrupted. "May I ask Mr. Sweet to please refrain from referring to Kelia Smith as a girl? She is twenty-two years old, Your Honor. She is a woman."

Omar continued. "Do you think a man who goes after a woman half his age, who moves into her parents' house, and lives off their food and goodwill, a man who has sex in the driveway in full view of the neighbors—Mr. Smith, do you think that that man is showing good judgment?"

"Leading!" Sloan shouted.

"I'll allow it," Judge Brand said.

"Of course that's not good judgment," George Smith said.

"Mr. Smith, what do you think it takes to be a good father?"

"Well, for starters you need your own house." He frowned at Roger. "And you need your own money." Clearly he was missing the point.

Omar gave him a gentle shove. "And do you think you need good judgment to be a good father?"

"Course you do. Good judgment and money and a house."

"Thank you, Mr. Smith. I'm done, Your Honor," Omar said.

The judge instructed Kelia's father to step down.

"Step down? I'm going back to work. Come on, honey." Pookie grabbed her bag and scuttled out behind her husband.

Judge Brand glanced at his watch. "Okay, who's up next?"

Things were moving more quickly than I'd imagined. Sloan handed the judge a large manila envelope. "Your honor, we believe that a child thrives in a home with two parents, a man and a woman. We have reason to believe that Miss Ryan is incapable of providing that kind of normal parental environment because of her sexual orientation." Brand leaned forward eagerly. "I submit these photographs for your consideration, Your Honor."

Here it comes.

Brand opened the envelope and slid out the pictures. He pushed his glasses up his nose and peered at the photos without expression. When he was through staring at them, Sloan set them on a small wooden easel. You could see one of Diana's breasts and her bare legs. I looked fat as a walrus. It didn't look like I was having sex with her. It looked like I was smothering her.

Sloan continued. "Your Honor, you are looking at an untouched and completely unaltered photograph of Valerie Ryan in bed with Diana Leland aka Diana Pierce, a known lesbian. Ms. Pierce is in the nude, your honor, as you can plainly see, and Ms. Ryan is lying on top of her. I believe it is safe to surmise that these two women are engaged in a sexually intimate act, sir."

"I wish!" The voice came from the back of the room. We all turned to watch Diana stride up the center aisle. She stood in front of the judge, hands on her hips. She was wearing a gray pinstriped pants suit, white shirt, and man's tie. "Your Honor, those pictures prove nothing. Valerie Ryan is not a lesbian. I should know. I've been after her for years!"

"And you are . . ." the judge asked.

"I guess you don't recognize me with my clothes on. I'm the woman in the picture. I'm Diana Leland Pierce."

Omar stood up. "Your honor, Ms. Leland is scheduled to testify later today. Would you have any objection to adjusting our schedule a bit so that Ms. Leland may speak now?"

Judge brand turned to Sloan and raised his eyebrows. "Do you have any problem with that?"

Sloan shrugged. "No, Your Honor."

The judge gestured toward the witness table. "Take a seat, Ms. Leland."

"Gladly, Your Honor." Diana hopped onto the platform and slid into the seat. She clasped her hands primly and waited for the first question.

Omar started by addressing Judge Brand. "Your Honor, Roger Tisdale's attorneys will argue that Valerie Ryan is unfit to be a mother because of her sexual orientation. I will set aside the implications of that premise for a moment—I am not here today to argue whether gay people can be competent, loving parents. I am here to refute the ridiculous and completely unwarranted claim that Valerie Ryan is a lesbian, and I've invited Ms. Leland to speak to that issue.

Omar approached the table. "Ms. Leland Pierce, for the record, are you a lesbian?"

Diana smiled. "Absolutely."

"You must admit that these photographs are rather damning, and yet you insist that Ms. Ryan is not a lesbian. Are you certain of that?"

"Yes, Mr. Sweet, I am. I can tell you with complete certainty that this woman"—she pointed at me, and smiled—"is not a lesbian. I'll admit it. I tricked her into meeting me at the motel. Then I sort of tugged at her and she lost her balance, which is why it appears that she is lying on me. She isn't. She fell on me and she's struggling to stand up." She turned to the judge. "Your Honor, Valerie has always been interested in men and only men. I'm the one who's interested in women, not Valerie Ryan." Diana fixed her gaze on Sloan's female assistant in the beautiful aubergine suit and winked at her. The young woman blushed and shuffled her papers.

Omar sighed and smiled knowingly. So, just to re-state, Valerie Ryan is not a lesbian, correct?"

"No. Mr. Sweet, Valerie Ryan is not a lesbian," Diana said. "Unfortunately."

The judge shook his head disdainfully and turned to Sloan. "Questions?"

"I have nothing for this witness, Your Honor," Sloan said. "However, I would like to state for the record that this photograph is highly suggestive, regardless of Ms. Pierce's testimony. The woman is in bed naked, Your Honor. Ms. Ryan is making bodily contact with her, Your Honor. The facts are there, in black-and-white."

Judge Brand took a deep breath and leaned back in his chair. "Mr. Sloan, I have little sympathy for those who practice deviant lifestyles. On this point I have made myself quite clear, and publicly so. But if the facts of Ms. Ryan's sexuality rest on this single photograph, you're skating on thin ice, Mr. Sloan. Unless you have stronger evidence to bolster your claim, I suggest that you abandon this line of argument. Ms. Pierce, uh, Ms. Leland, whatever it is, you may step down."

"With pleasure, Your Honor." Diana slid out of her seat and left the courtroom. Under other circumstances she would have smiled or given me the thumbs-up, but apparently she thought it best to minimize contact.

"You may call your next witness, Mr. Sweet."

"Thank you, Your Honor." Omar stood up. "At this point I'd like to call Alyssa Elkins to testify."

Alyssa moved slowly toward the witness table. I realized with joy in my heart that she looked like she has packed on the pounds. Not that she's ready to shop at Lane Giant, but her face was fuller and she was wearing a long blouse (a garment undoubtedly chosen for its high MBC—maximum butt coverage—index). Alyssa's hair was pulled back, and for the first time I noticed her enormous flapping ears. Welcome to the club, Chunky Monkey. Just wait until you have your first kid.

Omar sprung to his feet and straightened his tie. "Thank you for joining us today, Ms. Elkins. For the record, you aren't exactly thrilled to be here, are you?"

"No." Her eyes briefly met mine. She looked away quickly. She didn't look at Roger.

Omar turned to the judge. "I'd like to point out that Alyssa Elkins appears before Your Honor today not of her own free will, but because she has been subpoenaed to do so." Alyssa rolled her eyes. "We believe that her testimony will support our contention that Roger Tisdale is not fit to retain full custody of Peter Ryan Tisdale."

"Please continue," Brand said.

"Ms. Elkins, please describe, if you would, your relationship to Roger Tisdale."

Alyssa leaned forward. "I have no relationship to Roger Tisdale."

"Fair enough, Ms. Elkins. Would you please describe, then, your past relationship with Mr. Tisdale."

She smirked. "Roger was my teacher and my lover."

Interesting. I hadn't expected it to hurt but it did. Those two words—*my lover*—dredged up my worst memories quicker than a needleful of sodium pentathol. I could see Roger and Alyssa flirting outside the Learning Attic. I remembered finding her plastic diaphragm case in the van, and recalled all of Roger's crazy excuses ("She asked me to hold it for her. I swear!"). What hurt most, though, was remembering how badly I'd wanted to believe him, and how willing I was to overlook what I thought was his one and only transgression.

"Your teacher and your lover," Omar echoed, and the words stung just as sharply the second time around. "Ms. Elkins, you had a sexual relationship with Mr. Tisdale, then?"

"Yes, that's what I mean when I say he was my lover." (Yet again.)

"Will you tell us how you met Mr. Tisdale, please?"

"He was my teacher. At the Learning Attic. I took his class because I wanted to learn more about writing plays. I thought I had writing talent and I wanted an expert opinion."

"At what point did your relationship become sexual?"

"We started having sex almost right away." I didn't want to hear this. I looked at Kelia, who was furiously chewing her nails to the quick. "I could tell he liked me just by the way he looked at me. He'd leave notes on my papers like, 'See me after class.' Nobody else got notes like that. We started going for drinks after class. One night he offered to drive me home in his van even though I had my car. I mean, I was parked right there in front of the street and he knew it. I let him drive me home, figuring I could always go pick up my car the next day. He drove to Baker's Point, out by the old train tracks. He kissed me for the first time that night." She stopped and looked down at her fingernails. She looked as if she might cry. But her face quickly hardened and she continued. "He told me he was getting a divorce. And I was stupid enough to believe him."

Omar let the words hang there for a moment. Then he asked, "Ms. Elkins, did you know that Roger Tisdale had a son?"

"That first time in the van, I noticed the kiddy seat. But when I asked Roger about it, he said it was for his sister's kid. He said they were visiting from Atlanta and he borrowed the car seat from a neighbor. Lynette something."

"So," Omar continued, watching Judge Brand as he addressed Alyssa, "Roger Tisdale didn't want you to know that the car seat in the back of his van belonged to his own son."

"That's what I just said," Alyssa answered.

"At what point did you discover that Roger Tisdale did, in fact, have a child?"

"I called and I heard Pete in the background and he was screaming something like, 'Daddy, Daddy, look at me, Daddy.' So I asked him, Who's that? That's when he told me. He told me the truth. He really did have a son."

"Why do you suppose Mr. Tisdale kept it a secret from you?"

"He said he didn't want to scare me off. But I tried to tell him, I loved kids. I was an ed major. I wanted to teach kindergarten. I loved kids."

"Ms. Elkins, as someone with a background in early childhood development, you must have some sense of the qualities that make a good parent." Alyssa straightened up and assumed a squinty, studious look. "Do you believe that Roger Tisdale is a good father? I will remind you, Miss Elkins, that you are in a court of law, and you have already provided your sworn testimony in your deposition. So let me ask the question again. Do you believe that Roger Tisdale is a good father?"

Alyssa lifted her eyes and glanced at Roger. "No, I don't."

"And why not?" Omar prodded.

"Because a good father wouldn't leave his kid home alone the way Roger did. Hours at a time. While we were miles away. Having sex."

Omar folded his arms and tossed a disgusted glare at Roger. "Can you elaborate, please?"

Alyssa shifted uncomfortably in her seat. She pushed up the sleeves of her blouse and pushed them back down again. She cleared her throat. "Look. It was his idea. Not mine. I kept telling him it was a bad idea."

"Please continue, Miss Elkins," Omar said.

"It happened three or four times. Maybe five. His wife would work late. Roger would page me—he'd punch in 69, that was our little code—and that's how I knew to come over. In the meantime, he'd get Pete down for the night, read him a book, that kind of thing, and then when he was sure the kid was sound asleep— you know, when he was in his Alpha sleep, his REM sleep, whatever—he'd meet me out in the driveway and we'd take off. He always locked up the house, of course. And he left plenty of lights on so it looked like people were home. We'd go to Baker's Point or the Econolodge. We never went too far and we were always back within a couple of hours. But, I mean, we did leave Pete alone in the house. As far as we knew, he never woke up. But I still thought it was a bad idea. And I told him so."

Omar was quiet for a moment as Judge Brand absorbed the impact of Alyssa's testimony. I didn't quite know what to do with my outrage. It was so long ago, and Pete, thank God, was alive and well, in spite of Roger's negligence. I was left with a gnawing uneasiness. As much as I'd grown to distrust and despise Roger as a husband, I always believed that Roger was a dutiful father.

"No further questions," Omar said. He strode back to his seat.

Sloan jumped up. "Miss Elkins, is it true that you worked as a prostitute?"

She froze.

"Miss Elkins?"

"I was an escort, and I thought we weren't going to

talk about all that! You said we wouldn't have to talk about that!" She was yelling at Omar now.

The judge leaned forward eagerly. "Please answer the question, Miss Elkins."

She clenched her jaw. "I was an escort when I was in college. I did it to pay my tuition. Otherwise I wouldn't have been able to get my degree."

Sloan smirked. "I don't suppose you could have gotten a job flipping burgers or bagging groceries like other college kids?"

"Do you have any idea what tuition costs these days? Those kinds of jobs wouldn't have even paid for my textbooks, for your information."

"So, for the record, you offered sex in exchange for money, correct?"

Alyssa mumbled something.

Sloan rapped on the desk. "Speak up, please."

She shut her eyes. "I said, yes."

"Did my client know you were a prostitute? Er, excuse me, an *escort?*"

"I certainly wasn't going to tell him. But he found out anyway." Alyssa glared at me. "His wife told him. I mean, his ex-wife." Another greasy memory came gurgling up to the surface. Me and Dale at lunch. Alyssa walks in. Dale recognizes her from a party, tells me she's a hooker. That night I pray Roger hasn't contracted any communicable diseases.

"Your Honor," Sloan began, "I do hope you will consider this testimony in light of its source, a prostitute who has admitted here today that she lies when it suits her purposes. This young woman has been engaged in criminal as well as deceptive behavior, and I urge that her testimony be regarded with suspicion if it is to be regarded at all."

"Look," Alyssa said, "I'm not making any of this up. Roger left his son alone so we could go and—"

"That will be all, Miss Elkins," Sloan interrupted. "You can leave now. Thank you for your time."

"Wait a second—"

"I *said*, that will be all."

"Fine!" she snapped as she rose from her seat. "I'm leaving!" She pulled her blouse down around her hips and started for the door.

Lynette was next. She smiled tentatively at me as she nervously took her seat. I didn't think there would be any surprises. She would tell the soap-carving story and the fire-building story, and that would be the end of it. I hadn't expected her to tell about the time Pete burned his hand during the Tiger Cub camping trip. "We tried to call home, but the phone was off the hook," she reported quietly. "My husband told me later that Val had had a visitor that day. A man." Lynette looked at me apologetically.

I felt my stomach drop.

"Relevance?" Omar demanded.

Sloan raised his hands in the air. "It goes to the question of negligence, Your Honor. She had listed her home number in case of emergency, and yet there she was, entertaining male callers, and disconnecting her phone, knowing full well that there would be no way to reach her in the event of an emergency. Now, what kind of mother would do such a thing?"

Lynette jumped in. "But Valerie told me she had accidentally knocked the phone off the hook. That sort of thing happens all the time. I never said she disconnected the phone on purpose."

But I had done precisely that, I remembered with a guilty shiver. Eddie's wife had called. I hadn't wanted her to call again. I took the phone off the hook. I'd completely forgotten that Pete might need to reach me.

Judge Brand rubbed his eyes wearily. "Mr. Sloan, you are making a tenuous connection at best. Mrs. Chase, you are excused."

"Thank you, Your Honor," she said. Lynette gave me another one of her grief-stricken stares. I couldn't bear to look at her.

Omar squeezed my hand. "Don't panic," he whispered. "It's going great." And you know what? For a minute I actually agreed with him. For the first time since the hearing had begun, I'd actually allowed myself to feel optimistic. Until that point, I'd assumed the worst: I was going to wind up childless, penniless, homeless. Now Omar's confidence bolstered me like steel beams. I felt bulletproof. We were going to win this thing. I knew it.

Omar reached into his briefcase and pulled something out. "Your Honor, I'd like to move on to our next piece of testimony," he said. He was holding a video-tape.

I hadn't even noticed the VCR on our table until Omar slipped the videotape inside. My pulse pounded as he leaned across the table to switch on the TV. Omar pressed the play button on the VCR. There was nothing but deafening gray static. He fiddled with a few more buttons but no picture appeared. "Where are those nerdy A/V squad guys when you need them?" Omar muttered. Sloan rapped his pencil impatiently while Roger smirked. Kelia was still chewing her fingernails.

Omar haphazardly smacked a few more buttons. Finally a picture appeared on the screen. It was a woman, small but sturdy, perched on the edge of a tall kitchen stool. She wore a baggy black shirt and black pants, the nylon kind with many pockets and zippers and Velcro tabs. She held a cigarette between the thumb and index finger of her small hand, but over the next ten minutes, she never brought the cigarette to her lips, not once, not even when she appeared visibly distressed.

"Zoom in on me," she said. "No, not *that* button. The other one. I said, the *other* one." She rolled her eyes exasperatedly. "That's it. Get in close."

The voice had the authority of a Marine Corps sergeant. I knew that voice. It was Mary's aunt Esta. Now her face filled the TV screen. Her black hair was cut short, like a man's, and she wore a red beret at a rakish angle. Her face was shaped like a heart but her mouth was drawn and severe, a taut, lipless razor blade line.

Omar paused the tape. "Your Honor, at this point I would like to introduce the videotaped testimony of Ms. Esta Domingo. To quickly review, Roger Tisdale married Mary in a bogus ceremony, and kept her as a virtual prisoner in a condominium on Lake Merle. When confronted with his bigamy, Mr. Tisdale attempted to deny any relationship—actually, he attempted to deny any knowledge—of this girl. I believe that Esta Domingo's testimony will settle the question of whether Roger Tisdale deserves custody of Peter Ryan Tisdale." The judge nodded and Omar switched the tape back on.

Esta stared into the camera. "I'm sorry I cannot be there in person to testify. As I explained to Mr. Sweet, we are in the process of building a battered women's shelter and I am needed here.

"She didn't want to have sex with him," Esta continued, in a vaguely British accent. "But he filled her head with useless dreams. He said he would send her to nursing school someday. But the bastard never even registered her for bloody high school! What kind of bullshit is that?" Esta stabbed the air with her cigarette. "Roger Tisdale wasn't a husband. He was a man who liked young girls. He was a pig!"

I tried to read Brand's expression. He had the pained and disgusted look of a man with a bad case of gastroesophageal reflux. I found this encouraging. But I couldn't understand why Omar was so excited. There was no news here. Esta's testimony was already in the file.

Esta straightened her beret. "I suppose I should get to the matter at hand," she continued. "The issue, as I understand it, is whether or not Roger Tisdale is fit to be a father."

"Your Honor, this is ludicrous," Sloan complained wearily.

Judge Brand instructed Omar to pause the tape.

"Your Honor, by her own admission, this woman doesn't know Roger Tisdale," Sloan went on, rubbing his head. "She is not a child development expert. She knows nothing about the particulars of this case or the people involved. She is not qualified to address the issue of Roger Tisdale's paternal competence. I respectfully request that we go no further with this tape, Your Honor. For God's sake, Your Honor, do we really need to waste everyone's time with this crazy woman's testimony?"

"Sit down, Mr. Sloan."

"But Your Honor, this testimony is based on hearsay and puffery," Sloan whined, sounding very much like one of those fey prep school boys I'd known in graduate school. Actually, he sounded quite a bit like my ex-husband. "It's the biased testimony of a wacky paramilitary man-hating feminist." Sloan paused for dramatic effect and pulled out his trump card. "She is a *lesbian*, Your honor."

"Sit down, Mr. Sloan," the judge ordered. "And stay down. I want to see this tape. Please, Mr. Sweet."

"My pleasure, Your Honor." Omar hit the button again.

The frozen Esta was reanimated. "When Mary thought she was pregnant, she called me in desperation. She wanted an abortion. But it didn't make sense. Mary loved babies. She told me she had to do it for him. Roger Tisdale. He's the one who told her to get rid of the fetus. He told Mary he hated kids. I remember this precisely. Roger told Mary that children were a burden and a nuisance. He said kids just get in the way. He said he never even wanted Pete. He told Mary that if she goes through with the pregnancy, he would kill the baby himself, with his bare hands."

"Hearsay, Your Honor! This proves nothing, Your Honor!" Sloan interjected. Omar paused the tape.

"I believe I told you to shut up, Mr. Sloan." The judge turned to Omar. "Is that the gist of it, Mr. Sweet? Or does this witness have anything more substantive to say on this issue?"

"Yes, Your Honor. One more thing, if you'll indulge me just a moment longer, sir." He switched on the tape.

"Okay. Now. Get a wide-angle shot," Esta instructed. The unnamed cameraperson pulled back. Esta was holding something in her hands. It looked like a Dictaphone. "We always tape our phone conversations. House rule." Esta pressed a button and held the tiny machine in the air. "Okay. Zoom in again."

And then I heard Mary's voice, the childlike quaver,

the pleading desperation. "You have to help me, Auntie," Mary begged. I felt a lump rise in my throat. "Roger says I have to get rid of my baby. If I don't, he's going to kill it. He said he would come in the middle of the night and grab the baby by the throat and squeeze it dead with his own hands, Auntie! He swore it to God, Auntie! Oh, please, help me!" Esta clicked off the machine and stared into the camera. "So if you want to know whether Roger Tisdale would be a good father, I think you have your answer now."

"That's about the gist of it, Your Honor," Omar said. "After this point we're dealing with variations on a theme, sir."

"In that case, you may turn off the tape. I believe I've heard enough." Judge Brand removed his glasses and ran a hand over his face. He stood up. "Please be back in this courtroom in forty-five minutes."

Sloan and his assistants huddled among themselves. Omar reached for my hand and squeezed it. "Say a little prayer, Valerie. Not that we need it now. We've got this one in the bag."

Omar had enough confidence to dash out during Judge Brand's deliberations for a pint of hot and sour soup. I sat alone on a bench at the far end of the corridor, beneath the wide, dirty window, and felt the sun warm the back of my head.

I closed my eyes. I could hear Roger and Kelia talking—no, bickering. She must have told him to take deep cleansing breaths, or maybe she suggested he "be in the moment," because all of a sudden I heard him bark, "Cut the Buddhist crap, okay? I'm not one of your suburban housewife yoga morons," and she winced as if he had slapped her. Roger's tongue could sting sharper than any hand. Kelia must have discovered that by now.

And all I could think was, the bloom must be off the fucking rose. Now *she* can deal with Roger's sniping remarks, the cold wars, the public humiliations. I remembered the time we'd had some people over for dinner, Alexis something, a colleague from the Learning Attic, and her husband, Stephan, a classical pianist. We were sipping wine and talking about movies. I remember feeling unusually happy and relaxed. I happened to mention *Das Boat,* the one about German soldiers in a submarine.

"*Das Boat*?" Roger sneered. "You mean, *Das BOOT*?" He pronounced *boot* with a German accent, while I'd merely said Das Boat, half German, half English, the half-assed attempt of a girl who had never mastered languages, who had never traveled abroad, who felt like an algae among these cultured pearls of academia.

"Boot, boat, whatever." I hoped my husband wouldn't make a scene. "What do I know? I took Spanish."

"Okay, then, say boat in Spanish." Roger folded his arms and smiled at his friends.

After seven years of Spanish, I couldn't remember how to say boat. Crazy sounds and stray Spanish words bumbled in my head. *Película.* Manzana. Man of La Mancha. Chimichanga.

"I'm waiting, Señora Ryan."

I felt myself blush. I thought I heard Alexis giggle. And then a miracle happened. *"Barco,"* I said, amazed that I'd remembered, but also angry that I'd debased myself by indulging him in his cruel little game.

Roger clapped his hands. "Bravo! Now why don't you toddle into the *cocina* and fix us some *café?"* He tossed his head back and roared. Alexis and Stephan looked embarrassed for me.

I looked at my watch. The judge would be ready with his decision in six minutes. I began to torture myself with the possibility that Roger might have full custody of our son. What would I do? Then I remembered that little verse I learned in my brief stint with Overeaters Anonymous: God, grant me the serenity to accept the things I cannot change . . .

How had we gotten to this place? I remembered the joy on Roger's face when I called him into the bathroom to see the pregnancy test dip stick, which, by the way, he had matted and framed. I thought of the way he retrieved Ben & Jerry's fudge brownie frozen yogurt for me, just because I mentioned I had a hankering for it. How he massaged my swollen legs in those final weeks of pregnancy, how he kissed every toe and lettered each one: P-E-T-E-R and E-M-I-L-Y. We didn't know whether we were having a boy or a girl until Pete finally entered the world, and when he did, Roger cried like a baby himself.

Every promise and hope for the future, these were not idle promises or vain hopes, were they?

A cellophane-wrapped fortune cookie suddenly appeared in my lap. "Go ahead. See what the future holds." Omar towered above me, sleek as a fox and fully refreshed while I sat there like a sweaty Easter egg in Lynette's maternity jumper.

I unwrapped the cookie and cracked it open. It was empty. I stared into my lap. I felt like crying.

"Empty, huh?" He seemed to be suppressing a grimace. "Hey, you know what that means, don't you?"

"No, Omar, what does it mean?" I said, knowing he was making something up on the spot.

"That just means the possibilities are infinite."

"Really? I always thought it meant I was going to die."

"We're all going to die, Valerie. But I have a hunch you're not going anywhere anytime soon, and I'm just as confident that empty fortune cookies are not a reliable predictor of one's mortality—it just means someone was falling down on the job at the fortune cookie factory. So ease up on yourself, okay?" He squatted in front of me, and I marveled at his flexibility. My own legs were half as short and I couldn't spontaneously squat if you paid me. "Valerie?"

"What?"

"Listen to Uncle Omar. Everything will be fine." Omar looked at his watch and quickly sprung to his feet (equally impressive). "It's time." He grasped my hand and pulled me up. "Let's get in there before Judge Brand does. He hates waiting."

When we got back into the courtroom, Roger was already there but Kelia was not. Brand hoisted himself into his seat and cleared his throat. He looked tired. He shuffled and scanned some papers on his table. He took a deep breath and just stared, first at Roger, then at me. I wished I could read his mind. I wanted to get this over with.

"I'm not one of these judges who believes in the sacrosanct authority of all mothers," he began, and my heart sunk like an stone. "Yes, it's true that mother and child have a unique relationship. The mother carries and nurtures a child in her womb. She brings him into the world. She feeds him with her own body." Judge Brand leaned back in his chair and gazed at the ceiling as he continued. "But there is so much more to motherhood beyond this process of gestation and birth and the act of breast-feeding. Who answers the child's cries at night? Who creates a neat and orderly home for this child? Who gives him the spiritual and emotional guidance he needs to become a fine young man? Who?"

The judge paused and I fixated on the phrase "neat and orderly home." What, exactly, did he mean by that? Had someone told him that there have been petrified remnants of a Happy Meal in the back of my Jeep since

November? Did he know I've bought seven Phillips screwdrivers and can't find any of them? I prayed: God, if you give me full custody of Pete, I swear to you I will make a neat and orderly home for my son. I'll hang all my clothes at the end of the day, instead of heaping them on a chair. I will organize all the crap under the sink in the bathroom. I will find all my tools and keep them in a toolbox. Even better—I'll build a workshop in the garage with one of those pegboards with silhouettes of all the tools so you always know where everything goes. Dear God, please.

"Mr. Sloan," Judge Brand began, "when you and your client initially approached me for an ex parte hearing, you were working an angle, so to speak." Judge Brand leaned forward and clasped his hands. "You told me you had evidence that Ms. Ryan was in a sexual relationship with another woman. Specifically, that she had adopted a lesbian lifestyle. Mr. Sloan, I believe you chose this particular approach based on recent events in my own life, events that I have struggled to keep private. You attempted to use this information to your advantage. That was shoddy lawyering, Mr. Sloan. And as a strategy, it was a failure."

Roger held his head in his hands and rocked back and forth. Omar reached under the table and squeezed my hand.

The judge turned toward me. "Ms. Ryan, I have heard testimony today regarding your competence as a mother. I have heard about campfires and soap carvings and burned fingers, stories your ex-husband had hoped might support his case that you are unfit to retain full physical custody of Peter Ryan Tisdale."

Roger stopped rocking and began paying attention. He looked hopeful.

"But if I pulled children away from their parents every time some kid experimented with matches, there wouldn't be a child in this county living at home. They'd all be in foster care—and even then, they're going to explore the outer bounds of acceptable behavior. That's what kids do. And it doesn't make you a bad mother because Pete did it too."

In a rush of relief, and gratitude for the judge's kindness, I started to sob and once I started, I wasn't sure I'd be able to stop. This had been the nicest thing anyone had said about me in a very long time. Omar patted me on the back as I tried to pull myself together.

"Mr. Tisdale, I was prepared to judge this case solely on your merits as a father. I'd read your file. I knew you had a questionable history where the ladies are concerned, but I was prepared to set that aside for the purpose of determining custodial rights."

I held my breath. I think everyone in the room did.

"I changed my mind," Brand said. "After rereading your file, and hearing testimony in this courtroom today, I am convinced that your ability as a father is inextricably entwined with everything else in your life, with all the foul choices you've made as a husband, with your devious behavior, your shameless philandering, your puerile interest in young women, with your disgusting exploitation of a Filipina teenager."

Oh, joy! I wanted to grab Judge Brand and twirl him around the room. How I loved that man! But then his face darkened, and he looked toward me, and I knew I wasn't home free.

"Ms. Ryan, despite your husband's flagrantly decrepit behavior, I do believe that young Peter has every right to know his father. I'm doing this only for Peter's benefit, not Mr. Tisdale's—at this point I don't give a damn what Roger Tisdale wants. But Peter will flourish best if his father has some presence in his life, and that's a fact, whether or not you agree with me. So after careful deliberation—and with some reluctance, I must frankly add—I have decided to grant full physical custody to Valerie Ryan, and *supervised* visitation rights to Roger Tisdale. Mr. Tisdale, you may visit with Peter Ryan Tisdale on two Saturdays per month. Ms. Ryan will choose the specific dates at her discretion, and visits will take place at a location of Ms. Ryan's choosing. These visits will be supervised by Ms. Ryan or someone she appoints as her surrogate." Judge Brand smacked his gavel. "We are adjourned."

Omar grabbed me and wrapped me with his arms. "We did it!" he whispered, radiant with victory. I know I should have been happy. I was granted full physical custody of my son. And Pete would still have contact with his father, which, I suppose, was a good thing. But I'd hoped to slash Roger out of my life entirely, and now I would remain linked to him—and his assorted girlfriends—two precious Saturdays every month, for years and years and years to come. I wanted to cry.

When Pete got home, I hugged him long and hard. "You're choking me, Mommy."

"I'm sorry," I told him. "It's just that I really, really missed you today."

"What did the judge say?" he asked.

I pulled Pete onto my lap and kissed him on his neck, in that warm soft spot I love best. "Well, sweetie, the judge said that you will live here with me, and your dad can visit with you every other Saturday. How does that sound?"

Pete shrugged. "Okay, I guess," he muttered. He picked at a scab on his knuckles.

"And on those Saturdays when Dad visits, I can be there too!" I added.

"You mean, we'll be all together? Like a family?"

"Sort of," I said. "What do you think of that?"

Pete nodded. "Good."

At home there was a message waiting from my mother, and another from Bill Stropp. I didn't feel like talking to my mother, but I needed Bill as surely as a stiff drink.

'Til next time,

V

August 26

I called Bill back last night and was grateful that he hadn't asked about the custody hearing. He had only the sketchiest information about my life and I wanted to keep it that way. He knew I was divorced and he knew I had a child, and maybe he had a vague sense that I'd come into some money, but that was all. As far as I could tell, he knew nothing of Roger or his be-fouled reputation, and couldn't care less about my for-mer career as a therapist, or about my squandering of that career. We never talked about family or feelings, never probed the big existential questions or bothered to make small talk. And yet, our silent collusion created an intimacy deeper than any I'd ever known with any man. "I want to see you now," he said, and the serious-ness and restrained urgency in his voice took my breath away.

"I can't," I whispered, aware that Pete had reached the age of eavesdropping. "It's not that I don't want to. But I need to be home. I can't leave my son tonight."

"When does he go to sleep?"

"Nine, nine-thirty. Why do you ask?"

"Is he a sound sleeper?"

"Yes, usually," I said.

"Then let me come to you. Later tonight."

My heart hammered at my chest. I hadn't had a lover in the house since Eddie had insisted on helping me

search for Roger's gold. There were advantages to meeting at Bill's house. It sequestered the relationship safely
away from Pete, and I never had to worry what the
neighbors might think. "No one will see me," he said,
as if he'd read my thoughts. "Don't worry." When I
paused a moment longer, he growled, "I need you."

"Okay," I surrendered, wildly flattered to be the object of his desperate desire. "Make it later. Ten o'clock."

The line went dead and I realized he'd hung up.

I spent the rest of the evening doting on Pete, as I
slowly absorbed the full import of Judge Brand's ruling.
Pete was mine. I had sole physical and legal custody. I
would raise him without Roger's influence or interfer-
ence. I would make all of the religious, medical, educa-
tional, and ideological decisions affecting Pete's
upbringing. I have every reason to celebrate but I can't
help feeling as if I'd failed my son. Bottom line: Thanks
to me, he would be a little boy without a dad. According to some statistics, Pete was now more likely to
abuse drugs, drop out of school, and kill himself. I was
thrilled to have Roger out of my life, but I'm not sure
I've done my son any big favors.

By nine-thirty Pete was sleeping soundly. I showered,
pulled on a clean pair of stretch jeans and my favorite
top, a pale blue ribbed tank top. I spritzed myself with
the cologne I knew he liked, Victoria Secret's Angel. I
didn't want to slather on a lot of makeup, but wasn't
quite ready to let Bill see me barefaced, so I dabbed on
a bit of lip gloss.

By eleven o'clock, Bill still had not arrived. I called his house but no one answered. I figured he'd changed his mind, and I might have been insulted if I hadn't felt so exhausted. By 11:40 I was in bed, watching a rerun of *Taxi* and feeling sorry for myself. I clicked off the TV at midnight and drifted off to sleep.

I dreamt I was floating on my back in calm waters on a blue, sweet and sunny day. I was naked and completely comfortable. After a bit, I swam to shore and lay on a towel in the sand, and I could feel each droplet evaporate under wide, warm rays of a red sun. A muscular German shepherd approached and I intuitively knew that there was no reason to be afraid. I lay motionless as the dog lapped at my face, my eyes, my lips, my neck. I could feel his weight across my chest and I shifted my position to make myself more comfortable.

I opened my eyes. Bill Stropp was straddling me, gently peeling my tank top up over my breasts. He paid homage to one, then the other, and I thought I might still be dreaming, until he said, "You really should find another place to hide your key." I arched my back and let him lavish me with hot kisses. I was half asleep but fully aroused. Then I froze—what if Pete walked in? Again, Bill seemed to read my mind. "I locked the door." I wrapped my legs around his waist and took him in. He felt solid and strong and wild, and I felt the bed—no, the whole room—rock with the rhythm of our desire. Suddenly I could hear the robins in the linden trees at the side of the house and I realized we'd fallen asleep. The sun was rising. I opened my eyes to find him propped on an elbow, staring at me.

"You're beautiful," he said. "I stopped myself from asking, Who, me? "I'd better leave before your little one wakes up." The man really is a mind reader.

"Thanks," I said. I reached out and let my palm rest against his hard, flat belly. Immediately there was a stirring below. I withdrew my hand.

"Maybe we can go to the animal shelter later this week," he said.

"Huh?"

"To find you a dog."

"Then how will you slip into my house in the middle of the night?"

Bill smiled. "I wouldn't worry about that."

I lay back on the pillow and watched him pull his sweatpants over his strong legs. "I'll think about it. I don't know if I'm ready for another dependent." It was almost six o'clock. I almost offered to make him breakfast but changed my mind. Keep it clean and uncomplicated, I told myself.

Damn. It's almost midnight and I just remembered that Pete has a Tiger Club meeting after camp tomorrow and I still haven't sewn those badges to his shirt. I wonder if I can glue them on.

'Til next time,

V

August 27

Pete came home from his Tiger Cub meeting with a flier for the Dad n' Me camping trip. "Can Daddy take me?" Pete asked. "Can he?"

"Well, I don't know," I said.

"Why not?" I could tell he was poised for a meltdown.

"Wait a minute, Pete. I didn't say no. I said, I don't know. There's a difference." I wanted Pete to go camping, but I didn't want him alone with Roger. I'd have to find a surrogate to supervise him.

But who? My own father was dead, and I wasn't about to enlist my ex-father-in-law. "Pete, hon, I know you want an answer now but I can't give you one. I need to figure some stuff out."

"I knew it," he cried. "I'm going to be the only one there without a dad. It's not fair!" He grabbed a tile trivet off the kitchen counter, the one he'd painted himself at Hunter's birthday party, and smashed it to the floor.

I could feel the beginning of a migraine thundering at my temples. I bent down to pick up the pieces. "Help me with this," I asked. "Get me a paper bag from the cabinet."

"Get it yourself!" Pete screamed.

I was horrified. This was a side of Pete I'd rarely glimpsed. I knew the breakup had been hard on him—

it would be hard on any child. But I never imagined this transformation of character. I suppose I should be grateful that he's finally expressing his anger about the divorce. He's not sucking his thumb anymore, he's screaming at me and smashing trivets. I chased him upstairs and tried to talk to him but he'd locked himself into his room—another first. When he finally came downstairs he was calm and happy. I told him that divorce wasn't easy, and tried reassuring him that Dad and I both loved him, and that would never change. He nodded compliantly throughout my little monologue. I doubted he absorbed a single word.

I still need to find a surrogate for the camping trip. I'm completely stumped!

'Til next time,

V

August 28

I'm anxious to return to some semblance of a professional life. I don't need the money, obviously, but I find it painfully boring sitting at home while Pete is in school. Originally I thought it would be easy to fill the time. I'd work out at the club (or with the personal trainer I have yet to hire). I'd whip up delicious meals for Pete (who currently eats only four things: peanut butter, tortellini without sauce, toast with strawberry jelly, and dry cereal). I'd play all day with my friends

(Donna Gold is busy renovating her house, Lynette cleans all day, and I still don't feel entirely at ease with Diana).

I really want to work again. I can afford to open any store I'd like, but I'm not the retail type. It would be hard to go back to a staff job, dealing with the structure and pecking order, and all the duplicity and backbiting that comes with an office job. I decided to call Dale. Maybe we could go into practice together. The more I thought about it, the more I loved the idea.

"Hmmmmm," Dale mused. He paused. "Wait! I have a better idea! Oh my God, Val, you're going to love this!"

"What? What?" I asked.

"Buy the Center!"

"Excuse me?"

"I said, buy the Center! You have the money. I hear they're having some financial problems and they're shopping around for someone to take over operations. The hospital was considering it. But I heard the deal fell through."

I stopped breathing. Me? Buy the Center?

"Can you imagine the look on Cadence Bradley's face when they announce the new owner . . . and it's you?"

The idea was outrageous, deliciously wild. And very tempting.

'Til next time,

V

August 29

I'm too excited to sleep. The prospect of taking over the Center is too tantalizing to allow even a moment's rest. My brain starts buzzing every time I close my eyes so I've decided to abandon the notion of sleep, for now, and write instead.

Am I ready to reconnect with the Center? I'm not sure. There was a time when I believed that my sanity and dignity depended on making a clean break, starting fresh in a new career, or in no career, but never to rekindle my relationship with the Center. Now I'm considering the possibility that the best thing I can do for my sanity and dignity is to come full circle, to return to the place where my career flourished and eventually failed, to work peaceably with the woman who could hobble me with a frosty glare. Cadence Bradley, aka Amazon-dot-bitch, who could send me to the edge of despair with so little effort, an arched eyebrow, a flaring of the nostrils, a dismissive wave of her elegantly manicured hand. Her favorite and most transparently hostile technique was her silence. I'd walk into the room and she wouldn't even look up from her papers, let alone greet me. But as soon as anyone else arrived, she'd welcome him or her with uncharacteristic enthusiasm, as if to say, "Now *here's* someone worth greeting!"

There were more overt actions, of course. I'd show up at staff meetings and discover—judging from the

half-eaten platter of bagels and empty coffee cups—
that everyone else had shown up a good half hour before I did. It seems that Cadence had a habit of holding
a "meeting before the meeting," during which all the
critical decisions were discussed and resolved. By the
time I'd arrived she had worked her way to the bottom
of the agenda, and there was little left to discuss. Cadence had all kinds of excuses for excluding me, of
course. Sometimes she'd say, "I knew you'd be busy
with clients all morning." Or, "I tried to e-mail you with
the time change but it bounced back." Or, "I didn't
think the agenda would interest you." As our relationship deteriorated, she stopped bothering to concoct excuses. She simply froze me out.

Cadence had the territorial instincts of an un-
neutered dog; she wasn't shy about marking her terri-
tory. But her power plays were subtle, and if you didn't
know her, you might assume she was just trying to be
helpful. Once she appointed a psych major from the
university to serve as my intern; I hadn't asked for an
intern and, in fact, didn't want a college kid shadowing
me all day. I asked Cadence to transfer the girl to one of
the social workers, and she eventually did, but not
without a lot of huffing and eye rolling. Another time,
Cadence sent my secretary to a three-day computer-
training seminar, presumably to update her spread-
sheet skills. Unfortunately, Cadence never mentioned
the seminar to me, and she never hired a temp.

And I will never forget the time she suddenly canceled the Open Mind Fair—my brainchild—without warning me. I'd invested three years of my life developing Open Mind, a public forum designed to demystify mental illness. The fair had won two state awards and even a presidential distinction, yet none of that mattered to Cadence Bradley. In a matter of minutes, she had shut down Open Mind forever. She said she had no choice. Open Mind was unprofitable, and a drain on the Center's human resources. I knew the real reason: Cadence Bradley despised me.

I wasn't in a position to complain, though. Cadence may have had the social skills of a hyena, but there was no denying that the Center thrived under Cadence's fastidious leadership. She helped extend its reach to the north and south, cultivated strong relationships with the nine major regional hospitals, developed a decent Web site, and transformed the Center from a basically loosey-goosey operation to a serious, structured environment.

That seriousness and structure came at a cost. Until Cadence was hired, the Center was a lively, collegial workplace in which I felt generally respected and appreciated. When I spoke up at meetings, other therapists paid attention and my ideas (the Open Mind Fair, for instance) were often implemented. Cadence's arrival had a kind of dampening effect. When I raised new ideas, people reflexively looked to Cadence for her reaction first, and her reaction was either negative or nonexistent. Staff brainstorming stopped. Now Cadence devised the projects; the staff existed simply to execute her ideas. Consensus was no longer a goal. It didn't matter whether anyone agreed with Cadence. She had the power to unilaterally establish policies or abolish them, to initiate projects or terminate them.

And now I had the power to terminate Cadence Bradley . . . assuming I decide to buy the Center. And now, I've got to get some sleep or I'll be useless tomorrow.

'Til next time,

V

August 30

Diana called this morning to ask if I'd consider taking karate class with her. "It's a fabulous workout," she cooed, and I bristled at the suggestion that I needed to work out, even though I do. I hate it when other people imply what I already know for myself: I'm a blob.

"I don't know, Diana. Karate isn't exactly my style. I mean, I'm more the nonviolent type."

"Sure you are," she said with a chuckle.

"What's that supposed to mean?"

"Well, I know you like to think of yourself as a Ghandi type, but you know as well as I do that you'd pop Roger's balls with a knitting needle if you knew you could get away with it. And God only knows what you'd do to his little girlfriend."

She was right, of course. In fact, Roger isn't the only target of my roiling antipathy. I'd nurtured more than a few violent fantasies about Cadence and Alyssa.

"Besides, it's not about hurting people, it's about empowering yourself!" Diana urged.

"Yuck. I hate the word 'empowering'. It's so nineties."

"Fine. Then think of karate as strength training for the spirit. It's confidence building. You'll feel like a million bucks."

"I already feel like a million bucks. Millions and millions of bucks, in fact."

"Let me put it this way, then. The teacher is really cute and nice . . . and single."

"I've already got a nice guy in my life," I countered.

"No, Valerie, you've got a hard dick in your life. There's a difference."

Diana was right again. Bill Stropp was great in bed, but he wasn't exactly the marrying type. "Let me guess. He's single, and he's gay. Or he's single, and his ex-wife is a lunatic. Or they're both lunatics. Right?"

"Wrong. He's single and his wife's dead. And he never had kids because his late wife, may she rest in peace, had fertility problems. Okay?"

Now I felt guilty, yet oddly happy, which made me feel even more guilty.

"Oh, come on, Val. It'll be fun. Classes are at noon. Pete will be in school. You won't even need to hire a sitter. Come on. Please? Pretty pleeeeeze?"

She wore me down. I agreed to try a few classes, as long as I had the option of quitting if I really hated it. Actually, it wouldn't hurt to learn a little self-defense. And if I could lose a few pounds in the process, even better.

'Til next time,

𝒱

August 31

So I'm at the bagel place with Pete this morning, eating my usual (scrambled egg and Swiss cheese on a nicely browned every-seed bagel) and I'm feeling really sorry for myself because Bill Stropp is thinking about moving to Arizona. If he does, God only knows when I'll have sex again. I must have looked miserable, because Pete looked up from his King Arthur picture book and asked, "What's wrong, Mom? Are you thinking about Daddy?"

My son clings to the illusion that he might get to live with both parents someday, that Mom and Dad really love each other after all, that our divorce was just one big dumb mistake. I smiled and said, "I'm not really thinking about much of anything, sweetie."

As I picked the last of the seeds and salt off my plate and resolved to stay away from men for a while, I heard a loud "Ouch!" and turned to find a tall and rather adorable guy standing by the coffee counter, sucking his pinky. He saw me watching and pointed at the big pump. "That's hot coffee. Careful you don't burn yourself." His accent surprised me. He was British, or maybe South African, and his voice was warm and deep.

He sat inches away at the table beside mine. I tried not to stare. He had curly honey-colored hair, as thick as a boy's, though I'd peg him at about forty-three, maybe a bit older. His skin was deeply bronzed and the hair on his arms was bleached to the palest blond, nearly white, like a lifeguard's. He wore a softly faded indigo T-shirt and loose black cotton pants; he was built like someone whose living depended on a well-muscled body—a construction worker, maybe, or a farmer. There were laugh lines around eyes as blue as the Pacific, giving him a perpetual expression of delight, even when his face was in repose. There was intelligence in his eyes, and kindness, but also behind that, ferocity. His nose was prominent but not ungainly, his lips were generous. His teeth were bright and straight and there was a sexy little gap between the top front two. He had large, capable-looking hands and no wedding band, but I detected the slightest indentation around his ring finger where a wedding band might have been, a long time ago.

He caught me staring and smiled. He stood up to refill his cup and asked if I'd like more coffee. By that point I'd had enough caffeine to propel me through the ceiling. I said, "I'd love some." When he bent to take my cup I could smell his skin and it was fresh and clean, like rainwater. When he returned to his seat, the most bizarre feeling came over me. I felt I'd always known him, as if we were married in another life, as if there were a thread already linking us, fine as silk and resilient as a spider's web. The only thing we had between us was a smile, and yet I felt serene and happy and completely connected to this stranger.

I must be losing my mind.

He gestured toward Pete's book. "Ahhh, the great King Arthur," he said. He leaned closer and squinted at the page. "And, yes, there is his lovely Guinevere." He looked at me and I thought my head would combust.

Pete, who is normally reserved around strangers, looked up and smiled. "Do you like King Arthur?"

The man returned the smile. "Doesn't everyone?" He wiped a dab of cream cheese off his beautiful bottom lip. "After all, he did pull the sword from the stone when he was just a pip like you. Not even the strongest knight in the kingdom could accomplish such a feat."

Pete beamed at him, and though I'd just resolved to take a sabbatical from men, I felt I had to know his name and maybe, God willing, he would ask for my phone number. I wondered if he was thinking the same thing, because his eyes met mine and he started to open his mouth . . . and then Pete tugged my hand AND SAID HE HAD TO PEE! I rushed him to the bathroom, where pee turned into a more complicated ordeal (apparently his bagel and chocolate milk didn't exactly agree with him), and by the time I got out of the bathroom the adorable man with the British or South African accent was gone!

It figures.

'Til next time,

V

September 1

Well, I've taken the first step. I called Nancy Cooperman at Barlowe Associates and asked her to investigate the possibility of buying the Center. She wasn't especially encouraging. "There are better ways to spend your money," she said. "I can think of a dozen ways to maximize your return on investment, but buying the Center isn't one of them." I wanted to tell Nancy that this was about revenge, not return on investment. She wouldn't understand, so I kept it to myself.

"I'm sure you're right," I said. "But there are a lot of good people doing fine work there, and it would be a shame if they had to shut down just because they're strapped for cash."

Nancy didn't say anything at first, and I imagine she was weighing her options. If she acquiesced, she wouldn't be doing her job. But if she argued the point, she might lose me and all my money. It was a tricky situation and she'd have to handle me delicately, which she did.

"You have a point," she said. "Let me nose around and see what I can find out. Give me a few days, okay?"

"Fine, but I don't want to drag this out. I want to move quickly, before another buyer gets there before me," I said. While most of my crazy impulses become less attractive as time passes (buying a miniature horse, learning to speak Japanese, buying a fondue set, starting a day care center, dying my hair black), I'm more eager than ever to buy the Center. True, I don't know anything about operating a practice of that size (of any size, actually), but surely I can find the right people to help me.

"Nancy?"

"Yes, Valerie?"

"Please don't let anyone know you're working for me. Keep my name out of it. You've got my power of attorney, and as far as anyone's concerned, you're the only one they need to know right now."

"I understand," Nancy said. "I'll get back to you as soon as I know something."

September 4

Roger wants to see Pete this Saturday. I was hoping he'd be one of those absentee fathers you hear about on radio shows, the jerks who forget their kids' birthdays and call a couple of times a year if at all.

What a horrible thing to write! My son should have a

father who remembers his birthdays and calls every day, not once a year. But in order for Roger to remain involved in Pete's life, he must remain involved in my life too, which makes me feel claustrophobic.

I told Roger about the Tiger Cub camping trip, and suggested he save his visitation for that weekend. He was ecstatic until I mentioned that one of my male friends would have to supervise. "What kind of bullshit is this, Valerie?" he jabbed. "You think I'm going to try to kidnap my own kid?"

"I have no idea what you plan on doing with Peter," I said.

"Oh, now it's Peter?" he mimicked. "When did you start calling him Peter?"

"I don't have time for this, Roger."

"No. Really. Just tell me. When did Pete become Peter? Was that your idea? Or did that jackass Bill Stropp person suggest it?"

How the hell did he know about Bill Stropp??? "Roger," I said, trying to sound light and detached, "One of the great advantages of divorce is that I don't have to fight with you anymore. So if you'll excuse me, I need to go."

"Look. I'm sorry. I don't want to fight. This is hard for me, too, you know."

I didn't say anything.

"Please. Let me take Pete camping without the . . . supervision. Please. You can trust me, Val."

"I've got to go," I said, and hung up quickly, before he could squeeze another word in.

If being married to Roger was hard, being divorced from him may be even harder.

'Til next time,

cv

September 9

Michael Avila has agreed to accompany Pete on the Tiger Cubs camping trip. Now I have two weeks to develop some sort of relationship between them. I've invited Michael for dinner tonight. He asked if he could bring a date. I guess he's still convinced he can will himself to be heterosexual. Good luck, is all I can say.

Nancy Cooperman called to say that she talked to Tom France, general counsel for the Center. She told him about her anonymous client who is considering acquiring the Center and he seemed intrigued. He already had the prospectus from the last, albeit failed, negotiations with the hospital. I'll have a formal prospectus in my hands next week. "The asking price is about a million and a half," Nancy said.

"That's all? Are you sure?" Maybe I've already been jaded by my new wealth, but $1.5 million just didn't sound like a lot of money for a whole mental health practice.

"Well, I suppose I could convince them to take more," she said. It took a moment to realize she was being facetious.

I want to tell Dale but I've promised myself I won't tell a soul, not even my mother. If Cadence knows I'm behind this takeover, this deal is dead.

'Til next time,
V

September 10

Dinner with Michael went nicely. He came bearing Pokémon cards (including the apparently rare second edition hologram Alakazam card) and won Pete's heart. His date for the evening was Lorinda, a plump schoolteacher with bright blue eyes and a hearty laugh. She looked more like a beloved great-aunt than a girlfriend. They made an amiable, if bizarre-looking, couple.

'Til next time,
V

September 11

One of the tortures of being a parent, I've decided, is suffering through all the crap you thought you left behind. It's like some cruel karmic trick; just when you think you've transcended the teasing and rejection and humiliation (and math homework), your kid starts suffering through it himself, and when he suffers, you suffer. Whatever distance you may have gained growing older quickly narrows to a hair's breadth and you are transported right back there, back to grade school, back to the time Sharon Finley said you had the ugliest hair in second grade and, no, you can't play tetherball with her and Lisa Morgenstern because they're in a club and the club is called The Cool Girls Club and everyone is invited to join except Valerie Ryan because she has ugly hair.

And so you try your best to be wise and comforting when your kid comes home crying, but what you really want to say is, Just give me that brat's name and I will track him down and beat him within an inch of his life.

Pete came home in tears today. Apparently, Gregory James Martindale is having a serious birthday party—magician, clowns, ponies—and that little BASTARD invited EVERYBODY in class except for Pete. Gregory handed out his invitations IN SCHOOL, which isn't even ALLOWED, and for the rest of the day the kids were in an absolute frenzy.

To make matters worse, the Martindales' house is within spitting distance from ours; their backyard borders the creek behind our house, just east of Bill's property. When the trees become bare, we can see clearly into their yard. I'll have to make sure we're away that day.

When Pete came home crying. I wanted to cry along with him. Then I got mad. What kind of parents would allow this? I'd sooner cancel my party than allow Pete to deliberately reject one particular child. Then I realized why Pete had been excluded.

Gregory and Pete both play forward in soccer, but Greg never gets much time on the field because, frankly, he's a bit of a klutz. In fact, I'd asked Coach to give him more time on the field. This is a kids' league, for God's sake. Everyone deserves to play.

He listened politely, then said, "Soccer is serious business in this town. If you're looking for something less competitive, you could always sign Pete up for art classes or something. But that would be a shame, because your son is a damn good player. So why don't you just sit back and enjoy watching him play, and leave the coaching to me, okay?"

Last month the team played the Cougars, the best team in the league. Whoever won would advance to the countywide championship. Greg warmed the bench, as usual, while Pete played, and he played well. Near the end of the game, Coach decided to give Greg a chance, then yanked him out after two minutes and put Pete back in. Kippy was screaming and Greg Sr., who supposedly was a varsity basketball star in college, looked like he might rip the coach's head off.

And then Pete scored the winning goal and the crowd roared. The parents flooded the field and surrounded Pete, who was flushed with pride. My boy was a hero, while Gregory James had blown his big chance. I felt terrible for Greg.

After the game, I tried to say something to Kippy but she just glared at me while Greg Jr. repeatedly smashed his fist against the bleachers and wiped the tears off his face. I stupidly encouraged Pete to go over and talk to him, and he tried, but Greg spun around and waved his fist menacingly at Pete. "Go away," the boy screamed. "You suck!"

Greg Sr. marched over and put a hand on his son's shoulder. "It's not your fault," he said, loud enough for me to hear. "Coach feels sorry for Pete 'cause he comes from a broken home. He doesn't have a dad to play with him like you do."

I felt a knot of rage rise in my throat. "Excuse me?" I yelled. "What did you just say?"

He never turned around, but muttered, "You heard me."

I tried to be conciliatory. I caught up with him. "Look," I started. "I know this has to be painful for you, and I'm sorry about that, but—"

"Sorry?" he cut me off. "What do *you* have to be sorry about? Your kid is the biggest hog on the field! He's ruining it for everyone else!"

I wanted to say, Your kid's a lame-ass, and that's why Coach won't put him in! But as I stared at this sputtering, red-faced, hulking ex-jock, I knew the conversation was over. Diplomacy was a waste of time and hurling back insults would probably get me killed. So I took Pete's hand and walked away.

First I called Lynette to make sure there really was a

party. Yes, she said, Greg was having a party, and yes, there would be clowns, a pony, and a magician. Lynette had already heard that Pete was the only kid in the class who didn't get an invitation. "Poor little guy," she clucked sympathetically. "Hunter told me Greg made quite a scene handing out those darned invitations. He would never have gotten away with it if they hadn't had a sub today." Okay. That explains why Greg was allowed to pass out invitations during class time. Substitute teachers tend to be clueless, and also overly acquiescent.

I miraculously found the school directory in the kitchen drawer, which, in one of my organizing moods, I'd designated for phone books, and called Kippy Martindale. I'd hoped to convince her to reconsider. Pete was a mess. Surely we could put that silly soccer incident behind us and encourage the boys to be friends. But she wouldn't hear it. "I'm sorry, Valerie," she said, "but Gregory was very clear about this. He doesn't want Pete at his party. And I can't say that I blame him."

I swallowed hard. How I wished I could reach through the phone and strangle that woman. "Fine," I said. I hung up. I looked at Pete's hopeful face. "I'm sorry, sweetie," I told him. "I tried, but Greg and his mom aren't being very nice right now."

Pete wiped his eyes. "It's okay, Mom."

"Hey," I said, rubbing his back and wondering what it

would cost to buy Pete a pony, "maybe we can do something fun that day, just you and me. Where would you like to go? You name it." Pete started crying again, and with every heave of his bony chest I imagined smashing Kippy Martindale's highlighted head into the wall.

Spent all morning in Bill Stropp's bed, where he fed me strawberries and told me he'd decided to move out west to be closer to his kids. I wasn't devastated. I wasn't even sad. Somehow I always knew that Bill Stropp would be transitory and celestial, like an angel.

I told him I was going to take a karate class. He wrapped his hand around my biceps and squeezed. "Mmmmm . . ." he said. "You're going to be a toughie. I like that." He traced a finger across my lips and then kissed me, a deep and long kiss that made every nerve ending come alive. We had sex for the third time, lazily, playfully. I'm not even sure I came, but it didn't matter, because I felt so good, sleepy and warm and free. We both fell asleep, and when I woke up I kissed him for the last time. He would be moving and it was time for me to move on.

The second best thing that came of my morning with Bill (sex being the first) was a solution to the Gregory James Martindale birthday party problem. "Here's what you do," he said, pulling his jeans on. He wasn't wearing underwear, and this small detail reminded me why I've enjoyed knowing Bill Stropp these past few months. "Give Pete his own party."

"But it's not his birthday," I said.

"So what? Give him a party just for the hell of it," he said. In fact, have Pete's party on the same day, but make it noon to three. So what if the Martindales rent a couple of clowns and some loser pony. You hire the whole freakin' circus. Pete invites everyone in class, *except* Greg Martindale, who can watch Pete's kickass party from his backyard. How does that sound?"

I told him it sounded juvenile, but I secretly thought it was a wickedly delicious idea. "You don't like this kid very much, do you?" I asked.

"I caught him throwing rocks at my dog. I think he's a mean little bastard."

As I pulled out of Bill's driveway, I glanced at the Martindales' house, a white Cape Cod with black shutters and a small guest house at the side, designed to look like a stable. Then I saw her. Kippy Martindale. Standing at an upstairs window behind gauzy white curtains. She was watching me. Through binoculars! Now I realized how Roger knew about Bill. Kippy, hateful, vengeful, and bitter, must have told him! But why? Because of a stupid soccer game? Or did she have another reason for hating me?

I don't have time to figure this out. I've got a party to plan!

'Til next time,

V

September 12

Maybe money can't buy you love, but I've discovered that most everything else has a price tag. I called Alexi Chen at Perfect Parties in Chicago; I'd read about her in *People* magazine. Chen's clients are celebrities and urban aristocrats, not unemployed suburban soccer moms. Not surprisingly, she wasn't particularly solicitous when I called. Then I uttered those four magic words—*Money Is No Object*—and suddenly Alexi Chen was my best friend, chatty and interested and eager to please.

Alex assured me that she'd have some "smashing" ideas by Monday, and if I was willing to pay, the short deadline wouldn't be a problem. "Listen, Val," she said, as if she'd known me her whole life, "remember a certain concert that was canceled due to the singer's sudden illness? She wasn't ill. She was working for me. I paid her twice her fee at the Garden to sing at Stevie Spielberg's New Year's Eve party!"

Stevie Spielberg? I love it.

I can't wait to tell Pete. And, I've got to admit, I'm even more anxious for Pete to tell Gregory James Martindale that he's not invited to the mother of all parties.

'Til next time,

V

September 13

I changed my mind. It would be small-minded and immature to exclude Greg Martindale. I've got to sacrifice my vindictive impulses and make the responsible choice: the brat will get an invitation.

'Til next time,
V

September 15

Two major events today. I heard back from Alexi Chen about Pete's party, and Nancy Cooperman called with figures for the Center. I gave the go-ahead on both deals. Barring catastrophe, these are likely to be the two most spectacular purchases of my life. More later—I've got to whip up invitations on my computer.

'Til next time,
V

September 16

Gregory James Martindale will have Abner Cadabra at his party, a washed-up drunk whose tricks are so sloppy that even the youngest kids figure them out, and scream things like, "You've got it behind your back!" and most of them lose interest and wander away.

Our magician, on the other hand, will be David Copperfield. As for clowns, we've got six of them, replete with all their clownish paraphernalia, from the Big Apple Circus. And because no party is complete without music, Alexi hired Aaron Carter. Total package: $945,000, including airfare and entourage. A bargain.

I told Pete about his party. He thought I was kidding. Then I showed him the invitation and he went from stunned silence to hysterical ecstasy. He asked if we could invite his father and I told him yes, which doubled his joy. It seemed like an easy way to please my son while fulfilling the court-ordered supervised visitation.

The Center's price tag is $1.2 million. Nancy thinks that Tom France will accept $1 million based on the outdated condition of the facility (it will need a new heating and cooling system, a new sprinkler system, and construction for handicap-accessibility). Unexpected bonus: After doing some research, Nancy now believes that buying the Center is a promising investment—the Center is poised to become the outpatient facility for St. Agnes's Hospital, and more importantly, it's the only mental health care practice certified for HMO insurance coverage.

"Buy it," I instructed.

"Wouldn't you like to give it further consideration?" she asked.

"At least sleep on it?"

"Buy it, Nancy. Make it happen this week. I don't want to wait."

She paused. It was an interesting moment; I'm not accustomed to commanding. "Will do."

I asked her to arrange a private meeting with Cadence Bradley at 8:30 A.M. on Friday, and a second meeting with the trustees and executive staff at 9. "Only then," I said, "will these people find out who's behind the acquisition."

I've decided what I want to do with Cadence Bradley. Friday can't come soon enough.

'Til next time,

V

September 17

Diana called to remind me that our first karate class is next Monday. I think I'll have to beg off. Too much going on right now.

Pete passed out the invitations after school. Gregory James Martindale never even opened his. According to Pete, he just ripped it up and tossed it on the floor. "I'd never come to one of your stinkin' parties," he screamed, "you stupid dickhead!"

"Then everyone started sort of laughing because Greg called me a dickhead," Pete explained. "And then they started opening their invitations and nobody laughed anymore. They were screaming too hard. And then Miss Linda the bus aide yelled at me for making a commotion, but when I showed her the invitation she stated screaming too. And she asked if she could come to the party and I told her yes. Is that okay, Mom?"

"That's okay, Pete," I said, smoothing his hair. "That's just fine."

Nancy called. The Center is officially mine. She said she would drop off the keys and all the paperwork tonight.

'Til next time,

V

September 18

Tomorrow is my debut as the new executive director of the Westfield Center for Emotional Wellness. I'm going to wear my baby blue pants suit and new Prada pumps. The gods must be smiling: I've lost five and a half pounds!

'Til next time,

V

September 19

I arranged for Pete to spend the early morning at Lynette's, and arrived at the Center at 7 A.M., long before even the earliest of early birds. I waited in the conference room and reviewed the research Nancy had compiled. I needed to be entirely up to speed on the St. Agnes deal.

By 7:30 I began to doubt myself. What the hell was I doing? How could I possibly assume leadership of a mental health facility when I could barely sustain my own career? Why had I done this? Just for revenge on Cadence Bradley? Was it worth it?

Absolutely.

Cadence arrived at 8:25 with a coffee mug in one hand, her briefcase in the other. Her powder pink suit was magnificent. Her face still looked like Henry Kissinger. "What are *you* doing here?" she said, disdainful as ever.

"I'm scheduled for a meeting at 8:30," I said.

"Well, you're in the wrong place, because I'm here for a meeting, too, and it most certainly does not involve you."

"How can you be so sure?" I asked, loving every minute of this.

"Because my meeting involves the new executive director." She set her coffee down on the table. "So if you don't mind—"

"Now, *that's* a coincidence," I told her. "My meeting involves the new executive director too."

"That's not possible," she said with exasperation. "My meeting is a private meeting."

"So is mine," I said, smiling. "With you. I've acquired the Center. Cadence, I am your new executive director."

"You've got to be kidding," she said scornfully. "You? You couldn't manage a lemonade stand. This is all a big joke, right?"

I said nothing. Just then the delivery boy from Provence walked in with a huge platter of breakfast goodies. He looked at his slip. "Ms. Ryan? Can I get a signature please?"

I stood up. "Certainly."

Cadence grabbed her mug. "I resign. You'll have my letter this afternoon."

"Wait," I told her. "My first order of business was to give you a substantial raise. But I can't do that if you resign."

She stopped. "A raise?" She put her mug back on the table.

"Correct me if I'm wrong. We're paying you $140,000." Cadence pursed her lips and nodded ever so slightly. "Based on everything you've done to broaden the Center's geographic scope and boost revenues, I think a nice increase is in order. Don't you?"

She raised an eyebrow.

"I'm prepared to bring you up to $300,000, Cadence."

She peered at me suspiciously. "Why?"

"Because you deserve it."

"What's the catch?" she asked.

"No catch," I said. "But from now on, you'll be taking direction from me. And the first item on your docket is the Open Mind Fair. You shut it down. Now I'd like you to start it up again."

Cadence looked miserable. She was violently opposed to being my underling. But now she was making too much money to quit.

"Please have a plan for reviving Open Mind on my desk Monday morning," I told her.

"Fine," she said. "But where's your desk?"

"It's in your office. Or, should I say, what was formerly your office. I'm giving you the weekend to move your things out." I always loved the view from that office, and the way the sun shines through the windows in the morning. "I'll have a suitable space assigned to you by Monday."

What could she say? She was stuck. And I couldn't be happier.

'Til next time,

V

September 21

Tried to get out of tomorrow's karate class but Diana whined so pathetically that I gave in just to shut her up. "Just remember," I told her, "this is a test. This is only a test. If I don't like it, I can drop out, no hassles. Right?"

"Righty-oh," she said. "But I have a hunch you'll want to stay."

'Til next time,

V

September 22

My first day back at the Center went smoothly. I dropped Pete off at school, picked up an Egg McMuffin, and made it to my office by 9:15. I sat in on a couple of meetings, approved a new hire, and signed off on Cadence's proposal. It's now 11:30 and I'm about to leave for my karate class. Must run.

'Til next time,

V

September 22, *later*

The karate class was far more eventful than I'd expected.

The room was cavernous and smelled of sweat and vanilla air freshener, and the walls were mirrored. A sturdy-looking woman appeared. She looked older than my mother but was in better shape than me. "Welcome, everyone. I am Mrs. Snyder and I will be assisting today. Please take a moment to find a *gi* in your size."

She gestured toward a large cardboard box full of white uniforms in the corner of the room. "The dressing rooms are in the back. *Sensei* Scott will be with you in a moment."

Diana grabbed a size small, naturally. I took a

medium and hoped it would fit, which it did. "It suits you," she said, pulling her hair into a ponytail. "You look cute."

"I look like I'm wearing pajamas."

"You still look cute," she said. "Hurry up. Class is about to start." She left me alone in the dressing room. I hung my clothes up and set my shoes on a rack and took one last look in the mirror. I guess I did look kind of cute.

I was poised to leave the dressing room when I heard someone call out, "Line up, everyone. I am Sensei Scott and I am honored to welcome you today."

It was a familiar voice. The accent was British, maybe South African. My heart hammered as I stepped into the room. It was him! The rather adorable guy from the bagel place! He smiled delightedly when he saw me.

Then he mouthed something. Guinevere.

I think I'm going to like this class.

'Til next time,

𝒱

About the Author

Debra Kent writes the Diary of V for *Redbook* and Women.com and has contributed to such magazines as *Cosmopolitan, Family Circle, Mademoiselle* and *McCall's*. She lives with her husband and children in the Midwest.